HARLEQUIN
Presents

Welcome to this month's collection of Harlequin Presents! You'll be swept off your feet by our gorgeous heroes and their seductive ways.

First of all, be sure not to miss out on the next installment of THE ROYAL HOUSE OF NIROLI, *Bought by the Billionaire Prince* by Carol Marinelli. Ruthless rogue and rebel Luca Fierezza knows a scandal will end his chance to be king, but he can't stay away from supposed thief Megan Donovan. Sandra Marton's glamorous trilogy THE BILLIONAIRES' BRIDES also continues this month with *The Greek Prince's Chosen Wife*. Prince Damian Aristedes is shocked when he discovers Ivy is pregnant with his baby— and now he's not going to let her go. Next we have two sexy Italians to get your hearts pumping! In *Blackmailed into the Italian's Bed* by Miranda Lee, Gino Bortelli is back, and determined to have Jordan in his bed once again. In Kim Lawrence's *Claiming His Pregnant Wife*, Erin's marriage to Francesco quickly fell apart but she'll never be free of him—she's pregnant with his child! Meanwhile, in Carole Mortimer's *The Billionaire's Marriage Bargain*, Kenzie Masters is in a fix and needs the help of her estranged husband, Dominick—but it will come at a price.... In *The Brazilian Boss's Innocent Mistress* by Sarah Morgan, innocent Grace has to decide whether to settle her debts in Rafael Cordeiro's bed! And in *The Rich Man's Bride* by Catherine George, wealthy Ryder Wyndham is determined that career-minded Anna be his lady-of-the-manor bride! Finally, in *Bedded at His Convenience* by Margaret Mayo, Keisha believes Hunter has a strictly business offer, but soon discovers he has other ideas.... Happy reading!

*Chosen by him for business,
taken by him for pleasure…*

A classic collection of office romances from
Harlequin Presents by your favorite authors.

Available this month:

The Brazilian Boss's Innocent Mistress
by Sarah Morgan

Watch for more titles in this series coming soon!

Sarah Morgan

THE BRAZILIAN BOSS'S INNOCENT MISTRESS

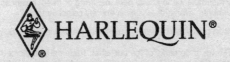

In Bed WITH THE Boss

HARLEQUIN®

TORONTO • NEW YORK • LONDON
AMSTERDAM • PARIS • SYDNEY • HAMBURG
STOCKHOLM • ATHENS • TOKYO • MILAN • MADRID
PRAGUE • WARSAW • BUDAPEST • AUCKLAND

ISBN-13: 978-0-373-12664-4
ISBN-10:   0-373-12664-6

THE BRAZILIAN BOSS'S INNOCENT MISTRESS

First North American Publication 2007.

Copyright © 2007 by Sarah Morgan.

www.eHarlequin.com

Printed in U.S.A.

All about the author...
Sarah Morgan

SARAH MORGAN was born in Wiltshire and
started writing at the age of eight when she
produced an autobiography of her hamster.

At the age of eighteen she traveled to London to
train as a nurse in one of London's top teaching
hospitals. She describes those years as extremely
happy and definitely censored! She worked in a
number of areas in the hospital after she qualified.

Over time her writing interests moved on from
hamsters to men, and she started creating romance
fiction. Her first completed manuscript, written
after the birth of her first child, was rejected
by Harlequin Books, but the comments were
encouraging, so she tried again. On the third
attempt her manuscript *Worth the Risk* was
accepted unchanged. She describes receiving the
acceptance letter as one of the best moments of
her life, after meeting her husband and having her
two children.

Sarah still works part-time in a health-related
industry and spends the rest of the time with her
family, trying to squeeze in writing whenever she
can. She is an enthusiastic skier and walker, and
loves outdoor life.

CHAPTER ONE

WHAT ON EARTH WAS SHE DOING HERE?

The helicopter swooped low over the trees and Grace felt her stomach roll.

Beneath her lay acres and acres of lush tropical rainforest, the canopy forming a dense green umbrella that sheltered and concealed the exotic mysteries of the forest floor. At any other time she would have been captivated by the wild, breathtaking beauty of her surroundings, but she was far too tense to think about anything except the meeting that lay ahead of her. The meeting and the man.

What on earth was she doing dressed in this ridiculously hot, scratchy suit, flying over the top of the Brazilian rainforest to throw herself at the mercy of a man who apparently didn't know the meaning of the word?

Rafael Cordeiro.

Brilliant, dangerous, *damaged.* So many words came to mind when thinking of him, none of them tame or soothing. Shockingly wealthy and wielding more power than kings and presidents, he was reputedly so clever with figures that the financial press had likened him to a walking computer. Which didn't bode well, Grace thought gloomily as she clutched at her seat, given her allergy to technology.

Beneath her, the trees parted and a swollen river snaked through a deep gorge and plunged over rocks in an explosion of white froth. 'He has properties all over the world—' she turned to the pilot, seeking answers to the questions bubbling in her mind '—so why is he living all the way out here?'

The pilot kept his eyes on the treetops. 'Because the world won't leave the man alone. He likes his privacy.'

Which fitted with what she'd heard about him. Ruthless, unemotional, unsentimental—the list of unflattering adjectives went on and on. Considering the man never gave interviews, there was no shortage of information on him. 'He's a loner?'

'Well, I wouldn't exactly call him soft and cuddly, if that's what you're asking, not that women seem to mind. Being bad and dangerous just seems to bring them flocking. That and the power. Women can sniff out power from a hundred paces. Power and money.' The pilot fingered the controls and then glanced towards her. 'You don't look like his usual type.'

His usual type?

Wondering how anyone could possibly mistake her for a billionaire's girlfriend, Grace almost laughed. 'I have a meeting with Mr Cordeiro. His company put up the original investment for my business.' *And that investment had changed her life.* 'He's what they call a business angel, but I expect you know that, given that you work for him.'

'Angel?' The pilot convulsed with laughter and the helicopter swooped alarmingly close to the treetops. 'Rafael Cordeiro—*angel?*'

'It's an expression. It means that he invests in small businesses that interest him.' And he'd been interested in hers. Until recently. The sick feeling in her stomach was suddenly back and Grace lifted her briefcase onto her lap and stroked the surface, trying to solder her fractured confidence.

The pilot was still laughing. 'Angel. I don't know what he

does to make his money but I can tell you one thing,' he fixed his gaze on the horizon and fiddled with the controls, 'the man is no angel.'

Refusing to let him frighten her, Grace straightened in her seat. 'I don't believe everything I read in the papers.'

'Obviously—' he glanced towards her and the smile on his craggy, weathered face was faintly pitying '—or you wouldn't be here. I can see you're a gutsy girl with a mind of your own and that's good, it will get you a long way out here in the jungle.'

'There's nothing gutsy about attending a business meeting.'

'That would depend on who you're doing business with.' The mountains rose and dipped and the helicopter swooped through a green-clad valley. 'And where. Not many people have the courage to visit the wolf in his lair.'

Despite her determination to keep an open mind, Grace felt her mouth dry. 'You call him the wolf?'

'Not me. That's what everyone else calls him. I just call him the boss.' His hands shifted on the controls and the helicopter lost height.

Losing her stomach and her nerve, Grace closed her eyes briefly and tried not to also lose her lunch. She'd never been any good on roller coasters. 'I'm sure Mr Cordeiro is a very reasonable man.'

'Are you?' He fixed his eyes on a spot far below them. 'Then you've obviously never met him. Hold on. We're going down.'

'Going down?' Grace stared at him in alarm, her worries about sickness and the dangers of Rafael Cordeiro momentarily eclipsed by that less than reassuring statement. 'Do you mean we're landing or we're crashing?'

But the pilot didn't answer. His eyes were narrowed and his jaw clenched as he played with the controls. For a moment it looked as though they were going to plunge into the trees and then, at the last minute, a small landing pad revealed itself and he lowered the machine down, landing like a giant insect in what seemed like a ridiculously small gap between the trees.

'Not crashing, then.' Grace gave a wobbly smile and let out the breath she'd been holding. 'I had a mental image of carnage.'

'If you're meeting with Cordeiro then there's going to be carnage.' The pilot flicked a switch in front of him. 'I've seen grown men in tears after five minutes with him. Take my advice and fight your corner. If there's one thing the boss hates, it's wimps. Welcome to the Atlantic rainforest, Miss Thacker. One of the most endangered little ecosystems on our planet.'

'You're leaving me? Here? In the middle of nowhere?' Grace turned her head and looked out of the window and only then did she see the lodge—a building that seemed to consist of nothing but glass domes and smooth, weathered wood, it blended into the forest so cleverly that it seemed almost to have grown naturally amongst the trees. 'Oh.' She looked at the walkways suspended high above the forest floor. 'It's stunning. Amazing.'

The pilot was laughing to himself. 'Rafael Cordeiro— angel.' Still chortling, he wiped a hand over his forehead and removed the beads of sweat. 'Out you get and keep your head down until you're clear of the blades. I'm flying back to Rio to pick up a package and then back to São Paulo.'

Grace sat glued to her seat, unwilling to abandon her last link with civilisation. 'You're not waiting? He said I could only have ten minutes…'

And it was completely ridiculous to have travelled all this way just for ten minutes, but what choice did she have? It was that or give up and there was no way she was giving up. Her one hope was that he'd agree to give her more time because she knew that ten minutes was never going to be enough time to dig herself out of the hole she'd fallen into.

'If there's anything left of you when he's finished, I'll come back and pick up the pieces. Take the walkway over there to the left and, whatever you do, don't stray off the path. This is the jungle, not a theme park. Watch out for the wildlife.'

'Wildlife?' She'd been too busy worrying about the meeting to even think about wildlife. She glanced dubiously into the dense forest that surrounded them. Some parts were in total shade whereas in others the sun penetrated the thick canopy of trees and was channelled onto the forest floor like spotlights. Was it her imagination or was it all moving? 'You mean insects?'

He gave a wicked smile. 'Over two thousand different species at the last estimation. And they're just the ones we know about.'

Trying not to think about all those legs scurrying towards her, Grace smoothed her skirt over her knees and wished she'd worn trousers. 'And snakes?'

'Oh, yes, there are snakes—' his grin widened as he glanced towards her thoroughly inadequate shoes '—and then there are the giant anteaters, jaguars and the—'

'OK, I think I've heard enough,' she said breathlessly, interrupting him with a shaky smile. *Any moment now she'd be clinging to his arm and begging him to fly her home.* 'I'm sure Mr Cordeiro wouldn't live here if it were that dangerous.'

The pilot threw back his head and laughed. 'You obviously don't know the first thing about him. He lives here *because* it's that dangerous, baby doll. He has a low boredom threshold. Likes to live life on the edge, so to speak.'

Baby doll? The careless way he'd diminished her to nothing irritated Grace sufficiently for her to forget her nerves. All her life she'd been patronised and underestimated. All her life people had doubted and dismissed her. And she'd proved them wrong, over and over again. She'd fought against the odds and she'd succeeded.

Until now.

Now she was in danger of losing everything she'd worked for.

And she wasn't going to let that happen.

This was probably the most important fight of her life and she was going to win. She *had* to win. And to win she had to forget that she was probably the worst person in the world to be given the responsibility of talking numbers with the Brazilian billionaire with the computer brain. She had to forget everything except the consequences of losing. *And the people depending on her.* If she failed then they lost their jobs, it was as simple as that.

If Rafael Cordeiro called in his loan, then it was all over.

The humid, oppressive heat wrapped itself around her like a thick, suffocating cloak and she pushed a damp strand of hair away from her face, her eyes drawn upwards, following the straight lines of the trees that rose to such impressive heights. It was like being in a remote, exotic paradise and it was hard to remember that cities like London and Rio de Janeiro even existed. 'Isn't he afraid, living out here?'

'Cordeiro?' The pilot chewed on a piece of gum and gave a grim smile. 'He isn't afraid of anything.'

Knowing that if she heard any more about the man she wouldn't have the courage to face him, let alone fight her corner, Grace stumbled out of the helicopter and discovered that her legs were shaking. At that precise moment she would have been hard pressed to say whether she was more afraid of the jungle or Rafael Cordeiro.

In a world obsessed with celebrity and image, he treated the notion of both with something approaching contempt, rejecting every invitation to talk about himself. And he didn't need to, because everyone else did the talking for him. The papers were full of curvaceous blondes who'd been persuaded to 'tell all' for the right amount of money. And so the whole world knew about his relentless pursuit of his billions, his prowess as a lover and his determined refusal to indulge in 'happy ever after'.

Once. Once he'd done that and the news of his glamorous wife's departure from his life after less than three months of wedded bliss had filled the newspapers with stories that had lasted longer than the marriage.

He'd been impossible to live with.

He'd ended their relationship by email.

He was only interested in making money. And more money.

The speculation had been endless but if any of it was to be believed then Rafael Cordeiro was little more than a machine and she knew, *she just knew,* even before she had to fight for her business, that he was going to be just the sort of man that brought out the worst in her.

She wouldn't look at him, she promised herself. If she didn't look at him she wouldn't become tongue-tied or stammer. She'd just pretend that she was in her small sitting room at home, talking to the mirror as she always did when she had an important presentation to memorise.

Grace felt her stomach lurch again and this time the feeling of sickness that enveloped her had nothing to do with the helicopter and everything to do with her past. At times like this—times that really mattered—the memories rolled up behind her like a giant wave, waiting to engulf her.

For her this was the ultimate test. And she wouldn't fail. She just couldn't.

Too much was at stake.

There was no reason to be afraid of Rafael Cordeiro, she assured herself as she stroked a hand over her straight, formal skirt and forced herself to move forward onto the wooden walkway that was suspended above the forest floor.

His personal life, no matter how dark, wasn't her concern. This meeting was about business and, whatever murk hovered around the man, he was a businessman, like her father. When she showed him her plans for taking the business into profit, he'd be positive. He'd change his mind about calling in the loan. She would save everyone's job and then she could fly home and leave the jaguars, the snakes and the billionaire Brazilian businessman to their jungle hideaway.

The tropical heat made her suit stick to her body and suddenly she realised just how woefully ill-prepared she was to meet this man. She wasn't even comfortable in her clothes. Stooping to free the spindly heel of her shoe from the careless bite of the wooden planks beneath her feet, Grace clutched the briefcase in her hand and suddenly wished she'd gone over the figures one more time in the helicopter.

But what difference would that have made? With the help of her father, she'd committed them to memory. There was nothing in her briefcase that wasn't already fixed in her mind.

Jerking her shoe from the jaws of the walkway, she regained her balance and straightened.

And saw him.

He stood directly in front of her, as dark and dangerous as anything that might have prowled out of the jungle, his body completely still, his eyes watchful.

And he was watching *her.*

Entirely unprepared for the physical impact of the man, Grace ceased to breathe. The helicopter, the rainforest and all her problems just seemed to melt into the background and she was conscious only of him.

His tarnished reputation had caused her mind to conjure up physical images that were so far removed from reality that for a moment Grace couldn't do anything except stare, as hundreds of women had undoubtedly stared before her.

His eyes locked on hers with the lethal accuracy of a deadly weapon and the breath left her body and every thought was sucked from her mind. For a wildly unsettling moment she couldn't remember anything about herself. She couldn't remember what she was doing here. Her body felt strangely lethargic and warmth as thick as treacle spread slowly through her limbs.

'Miss Thacker?' The hard bite of his deep, masculine voice was sufficient to wake her from her dreamy contemplation of his manly attributes and she gave a little start, desperately hoping that he hadn't noticed her embarrassing reaction.

So much for being cool and businesslike, she thought. And so much for her plan not to look at him. His physical presence and his film-star looks demanded attention. As she stood there gaping, it was a struggle to remind herself that this man was said to be ruthless and cold-hearted. For her, that wasn't a winning combination of character traits.

Looking into his deep-set, cynical eyes, she decided that there was something about his cool scrutiny that made him more menacing and intimidating than all the jungle predators put together and she knew in an instant that his pilot had been telling the truth about one thing—this man was no angel.

Forcing her legs to move, she walked towards him, her brief-case in one hand, the other seeking the reassurance of the rough rope handrail.

Even without the benefit of billions of dollars, Rafael Cordeiro would have attracted women. His hair was blue-black and swept back from a face that was as hard as it was handsome. The golden sheen of his bronzed skin betrayed his Brazilian heritage and the soft fabric of his casual shirt clung to shoulders that were wide and powerful.

She watched for his reaction to her arrival but he revealed nothing. His mouth didn't shift into a smile and his eyes, so dark and brooding, showed no sign of welcome. It seemed that he was as unfriendly as he was handsome and the way he was looking at her made her want to sprint back up the walkway and leap into the departing helicopter.

If she hadn't known better she would have thought she'd

upset him in some way but she knew that wasn't possible. How could she possibly have upset him? He'd never even met her before. His animosity was a reflection of his personality, rather than their relationship. He just wasn't a people person. And clearly he wasn't about to make an exception for her.

And it didn't matter, she told herself firmly.

She didn't need him to like her. She just needed him to agree not to withdraw his finance. Keeping that in mind, she took the last few steps until she was standing directly in front of him. 'It's a pleasure to meet you, Mr Cordeiro.'

His mouth tightened and his eyes gleamed with impatience. 'This isn't a social visit or a children's party, Miss Thacker. I don't want or expect polite. I don't do small talk or pleasantries. I don't care about the weather or the nature of your journey. If you find that approach to business challenging, then you'd better leave now.'

And a good afternoon to you, too, she thought, trying to hide her mounting dismay.

Suddenly she wanted to do precisely as he suggested. Staring into those deadly, dark eyes, she really, *really* wanted to leave. But the helicopter was already far above them and the reason for her visit was still safely stowed away in her briefcase. She couldn't leave. She had a job to do.

People depending on her.

'I can do facts and figures,' she said quickly, hoping that he couldn't see that her legs were shaking. 'I have all the documents in my briefcase. Everything you'll need to help you make a decision.'

'I've already made a decision. My answer is no.' His jaw was roughened by dark stubble and she watched as a muscle flickered in his lean cheek.

'But you made that decision before you had a chance to talk to me.' She wiped a damp hand over her skirt, refusing to allow him to squash her natural optimism. 'I'm hoping that once I've explained what's happening, you might rethink.'

'Why would I do that?'

Unease blossomed to life inside her. 'Once you see the figures and our plans for the future, I thought you might change your mind about withdrawing the finance.' She watched his face hopefully, searching for something—*anything*—that might indicate that he was receptive to further negotiation on the topic. Anything that might indicate that she hadn't wasted her time coming here.

But he didn't answer. He gave her no reassurance or encouragement. No hope at all. He just watched her and from behind her in the trees came a sharp wail, followed by what sounded like maniacal laughter.

Grace turned her head and squinted into the dense forest that surrounded them. With the helicopter gone she was suddenly aware of the constant background noise that enveloped them. Jungle sounds. Yelps, calls, shrieks, chirping and warbling. It was as if the whole forest was alive. 'It sounds as though someone is being murdered out there.' Laughter in her eyes, she looked back at him, seeking to build an emotional connection and falling at the first hurdle.

There was no connection. No answering smile. And it was impossible to know what he was thinking because his face revealed none of his thoughts.

'You're afraid of the jungle, Miss Thacker?' His tone was less than encouraging. 'Or is it something else that is making you nervous?'

Something else? Like the fact that her whole life was on the verge of being ground into the dust, perhaps, or the fact that she was alone in the rainforest with a man who obviously disliked the entire human race?

There were so many things to make her nervous she

wouldn't have known where to begin her list, but he wasn't exactly a man who invited confidences so Grace pushed away the mental image of the jaguars, snakes and two thousand species of insect. 'I'm not nervous—'

'Is that right?' He watched her for a few moments and then narrowed his eyes. 'Then let me give you a few more hints on how to do business with me. Don't waste my time, don't lie to me and most of all, don't cheat. They're the three things guaranteed to irritate me and I never say yes to anything when I'm irritated.'

What did women see in him? He was wrapped in a cloak of cynicism so thick that it didn't allow even the faintest chink of light to pass through and his eyes shimmered with an impatience that he didn't bother to mask with the usual social pleasantries.

'I won't lie to you. I don't lie to anyone.'

But she hadn't been absolutely honest with him either, had she? She hadn't revealed everything about herself when she'd taken up his loan. Discomfort and guilt slithered down her spine and she quickly reminded herself that there was nothing in the contract that stipulated that she tell everything about herself. And none of her personal history had any relevance to her ability to run her company—she'd made sure of it. Nevertheless she felt betraying colour touch her cheeks and saw him smile.

Just a flicker and not a particularly nice smile, but a definite indication that he'd seen her blush and filed it away as a point against her. 'You're a woman, Miss Thacker. Lying and cheating is welded into your DNA and you can't change that. The best we can hope for is that you endeavour to fight against thousands of years of evolution when you're in my company.' He pulled open the door and stood to one side so that she could pass through.

For a moment she just stood there, looking at him. 'Don't bully me, Mr Cordeiro.' Her voice was husky and shook slightly but she forced herself to carry on speaking. 'My business isn't doing well and I know we have things to discuss, but don't try and intimidate me.'

Never again was she allowing that to happen.

'Do I intimidate you?'

She was willing to bet he scared everyone he met. 'I think you could at least try to be a little more friendly.'

'Friendly?' His voice was faintly mocking. 'You want me to be *friendly?*'

She forced herself to hold his gaze. 'I just don't see why a business meeting always has to be cold and impersonal.'

He moved towards her and she took an instinctive step backwards. 'You want to get personal with me, Miss Thacker?' His lashes lowered, his eyes grazed hers and the heat and the humidity in the air rose to stifling proportions. 'How personal?' He moved closer still and she found it suddenly hard to breathe.

He wasn't touching her and yet her body was overwhelmingly conscious of every inch of his, as if it had been sleeping for the past twenty-three years and had suddenly been brought to life. 'I'm just trying to say that I've always felt that business can be fun as well as hard work.'

'Is that right?' He studied her for a long moment. 'Well, your attitude explains a great deal about the current state of your company accounts.'

He moved away but it took a few moments for her breathing to normalise and her heart rate to slow to something approximating its normal rhythm.

She wanted to respond to his less than flattering comment about her company, but he didn't give her the opportunity. Instead he strolled through the open door, leaving her to follow.

No wonder his wife left him, she thought miserably as she followed him, carefully closing the door between her and the jungle. Or was he arrogant and cynical *because* his wife had left?

As she pondered that question, it took her a moment to be aware of her surroundings but when she finally glanced around her she realised with a jolt of surprise that they hadn't left the rainforest outside at all. It was part of the lodge.

Following him through a huge glass dome, she glanced left and right, her attention caught by the profusion of huge, exotic plants that turned his home from amazing to spectacular. And through the glass, the rainforest, so close that inside and outside appeared to merge in perfect harmony.

At any other time she would have been fascinated, but it was obvious from his less than encouraging body language that Rafael Cordeiro had absolutely no interest in her opinion on his choice of home.

Making no attempt to put her at her ease, he led her into another large room and waved a hand towards a large round table that housed a state-of-the-art computer and several screens. Two phones were ringing but they both suddenly stopped, as if they'd been answered elsewhere. 'Sit down.'

Technology, Grace thought, eyeing the phones. He clearly wasn't as alone as he appeared to be.

She sank onto the nearest chair and glanced around her in awe. Through giant hexagonal panes of glass, the lush, dense greenery of the jungle pressed in on them.

'It's amazing,' she breathed, genuinely taken aback by the unusual nature of their surroundings. 'It's like sitting in a greenhouse in the middle of the forest.' Her eyes slid to a patch of fern that she saw moving. 'Do the animals come close? Do they know you're here?'

'Predators always sense their prey, Miss Thacker.' Rafael Cordeiro spoke in a low drawl, his accent so faint that it was barely detectable. He lounged back in his seat and lifted an eyebrow in expectation. 'I agreed to give you ten minutes. The clock starts now.'

Unprepared for such an unsympathetic approach, she gaped at him. 'You were serious? You really meant it when you said I could only have ten minutes?'

'I'm a busy man. And I never say anything I don't mean.'

He obviously wasn't going to make this easy for her.

Flustered by his total indifference to her dire predicament, she took a moment to gather her thoughts. 'All right. Well, you know why I'm here. Five years ago your company lent me the money to start up my business. Now you want to foreclose on the loan.'

'Don't waste time stating irrefutable facts,' he advised in a silky tone, his eyes flickering to the clock in an explicit reminder of his terms. 'You now have nine minutes remaining.'

She felt a flicker of panic. He was completely unreceptive. *She was wasting her time.* 'The business is important to me. It's everything.' Immediately she regretted that impulsive confession. Why would he be interested in the emotional stake that she had in the business?

Clearly he was wondering the same thing because his bold brows drew together in a discouraging frown. 'I'm interested in facts and figures. And you now have eight minutes remaining.'

She flushed and forced herself to plough on. *Don't get emotional, Grace. Don't get emotional.* 'As you know, I started a chain of coffee shops with your investment, but they're not just coffee shops.' She dropped her hands into her lap so that he couldn't see them shaking. 'We don't just sell a cup of coffee, we sell a whole Brazilian experience.'

'And just what constitutes a "Brazilian experience", Miss Thacker?' He lingered over the words and she bit her lip, refusing to allow him to intimidate her.

This was her baby, she reminded herself. She had all the answers she was going to need. 'People who come into our cafés are given far more than a shot of caffeine. For as long as it takes them to drink their coffee or eat their lunch, they're transported to Brazil. With your initial investment we opened twenty coffee shops across London. We're ready to open more, but not if you withdraw your support…' She broke off and rose to her feet, needing to pace. She couldn't sit across the table looking at that handsome face. *She couldn't concentrate.* 'Do you mind if I walk around? I'm not great at sitting at tables and if I only have a short time I have to be comfortable or I won't be able to make the most of it.'

His sardonic gaze slid to her feet. 'Frankly I'm amazed you can stand, let alone walk around. I see you gave careful thought to the footwear that would be most appropriate for a visit to the rainforest.'

Trying to keep her thoughts together, she refused to allow his sarcasm to unsettle her. 'This is a business meeting, Mr Cordeiro,' she said defensively, 'so I chose my clothing accordingly. I didn't think you'd take me seriously if I was wearing a pair of combat trousers.' Pride prevented her from confessing that both the shoes and the suit had been purchased specifically for this meeting.

Suddenly she felt like an idiot for thinking that what she wore would make a difference to a man like him.

Clearly she should have saved her money.

He was watching her closely. 'You mean you thought that a pair of sexy heels might make me change my mind about pulling out of the investment.' His voice was soft and deadly. 'You may have misunderstood my reputation, Miss Thacker. I keep my women and my business separate.' His gaze shifted to hers and she stared at him, unable to speak or move, caught in the dangerous heat of his gaze. Her body felt as though it had turned to liquid and a strange and unfamiliar warmth spread across her pelvis.

His women.

A clear vision filled her head and she saw Rafael Cordeiro

lying naked and bronzed on white silk sheets, his body damp after an excess of physical activity, an exhausted and deliriously grateful girl lying limp and sated by his side.

The vision shocked and unsettled her and she looked away for a moment, concentrating on the lush green of the jungle instead of the diamond-hard glint of his eyes.

'Miss Thacker?' His sharp prompt made her start and she turned her head and gave him a desperate look, hating herself for wondering how those long, bronzed fingers would feel on her flesh. What was the matter with her? She wasn't the sort of woman who mentally undressed men the moment she met them.

Especially not men like him.

He wasn't going to yield or compromise, she could see that. There was no softening, no gentleness and not a trace of warmth or humanity. For a terrifying moment she felt her confidence begin to crumble. The horribly familiar waves of panic began to engulf her and she dug her nails hard into her palms and looked away from him, staring at the trees for a moment while she struggled for composure.

You can do this, Grace, she told herself desperately. *You don't need him to make it easy for you.*

Since when had anyone *ever* made it easy for her?

Her entire life had been a struggle to prove herself and she wasn't expecting this encounter to be any different.

She used a precious thirty seconds of her time in calming herself and then she spoke. 'I wore the heels because they seemed right with the suit,' she said calmly, fighting against the sudden tension in the atmosphere. 'And you owe me another minute of time.'

He leaned back in his chair, his eyes narrowed. 'I do?'

'Yes, because that's how much time *you* just wasted talking about women's clothing.'

There was a long, pulsing silence and then he inclined his head. 'You still have eight minutes remaining.'

Grace started to breathe again. 'Good. The only thing I want from you is an opportunity to present the facts. I came here because I want to change your mind.'

She wished, desperately, that he wouldn't look at her but his gaze was unrelenting and she found it almost impossible to concentrate. The connection between them was electrically charged.

Did he feel it too? *Did he feel the heat and the rising tension?*

'I've already told you that I don't change my mind.'

'You also told me that you wanted facts and you haven't had them yet.' Her heart was thudding so hard she was certain that he must be able to hear it. 'You promised me ten minutes, Mr Cordeiro. My ten minutes isn't up.' And she was blowing the whole thing, she knew she was. It was all very well pretending to be confident but her knees were shaking, her hands were shaking, she was saying all the wrong things, letting one superior glance from those dark eyes turn her into a stuttering wreck. And he obviously recognised the effect he was having on her because he gave a silky smile.

'Nervous, Miss Thacker?'

'Of course I'm nervous…' She spread her hands in a gesture that pleaded for understanding—some concession on his part. 'In the circumstances, that's understandable, don't you think?'

At that precise moment, he was in the driving seat and she was standing in the road waiting to be run over.

'Absolutely.' His voice was as hard as his gaze was unsympathetic. 'In your position I'd be quaking in my boots and I'd be using every trick in the book to try and save myself, even down to the high heels, the innocent smile and the shiny hair. Go for it, I say.'

'I don't understand what you're implying.' Did he realise how uncomfortable she was in the shoes and the heels? Did he know that she'd been trying to impress him?

'I'm saying that your business is in serious trouble, Miss Thacker, and I'm the only one who can save it so I don't blame you for using every trick at your disposal to try and turn the tide. But I ought to warn you that it won't make any difference. I won't extend my investment and as far as I'm concerned you deserve everything that's coming to you.'

His callous lack of sentiment was like a vicious punch in the stomach.

'How can you say that? How can you be so uncaring?' She forgot her resolution not to get emotional. 'This isn't just about me. If Café Brazil goes under then lots of people are going to lose their jobs.'

'And you're terribly concerned about other people's welfare, are you not?'

There was something in his tone that increased her feeling of unease. Why did she have the sense that there were two conversations going on here? One above the surface and one below. 'Yes, actually. I think being an employer is a big responsibility. You can't just hire and fire people. I've been very careful about not recruiting more staff until we were sure that the business could support them.'

He raised an eyebrow. 'Very laudable, I'm sure. So what went wrong, Miss Thacker? If you're so careful, then why are you here? Why isn't your little business raking in the cash as we speak?'

'Our operating costs were higher than we'd estimated,' she said honestly, frowning slightly as she caught the cynical gleam in his eyes. 'Among other things, refurbishing ten of the coffee shops cost more than we planned. But we've addressed that and I have lots of ideas for the future.'

He watched her for a moment and the atmosphere thickened between them. 'You're very determined,' he said softly. 'Just how desperate are you?'

Grace stared at him, her mouth dry. What did he mean by

that? 'I care, Mr Cordeiro, if that's what you mean.' Refusing to be daunted, she took a deep breath and gave a shaky smile. 'I still have five minutes left to persuade you.'

She reached for her briefcase and removed the papers that she'd stowed carefully inside. Rafael Cordeiro was a man incapable of emotion so she had to appeal to a different part of him. He was a figures man so she'd give him figures. 'You won't continue your investment because, so far, you haven't seen a profit. But the cafés are doing well. Speculate to accumulate, isn't that what they say?'

'Do they?'

She flushed and forced herself to carry on and not be put off by his bored tone or the dangerous glint in his eyes. 'We're breaking even now and we'll soon be making money.'

'Is that right?'

Something in the way he was looking at her caused her feeling of unease to rocket. 'Once we start making money you'll also start making money...' Her voice tailed off as she saw the grim set of his mouth. *What did it take to make the man smile?* 'I'm going to be completely honest here. It's taken longer than I thought it would and the figures aren't what they should be. The cafés are all so busy that I can't understand why we're not already in profit.'

'Can you not?'

Faintly encouraged by his smooth tone, she decided to be completely open. 'I probably made a few mistakes at the beginning. Our operating costs were too high. Much higher than I planned. I paid more for things than I should have done. Now that we're expanding, it's easier to negotiate good deals. Give me a bit longer. You won't regret it.'

'I already regret it. I don't like the way you do business, Miss Thacker.'

Shocked, she stared at him. 'You mean, because the business

has been slow to take off? All right, I accept that, but give me a little longer. I have loads of ideas that I want to talk to you about. I know that I can make Café Brazil profitable.'

'But at whose expense, Miss Thacker?' His softly spoken question made her frown.

He was a billionaire. Surely the fact that she hadn't yet given him a financial return on his investment couldn't be that much of a problem? 'I realise that you've given us an enormous sum of money but we will pay it back with interest as the business grows. I'd really appreciate an opportunity to go through the figures with you and show you our plans. I really hope that when I've given you a full picture of where we're going with Café Brazil, you'll agree to extend your investment.'

'Why would I do that?'

'Because you'll see that it's worth it for you.' She lifted her briefcase onto the table. 'If you withdraw your investment then the company goes under, it's as simple as that. And if the company goes under—'

'You lose your enviable lifestyle.'

She frowned slightly, thinking of the fourteen-hour days she'd been putting into the business. Was that what he meant? 'I'm certainly lucky to have a business that I love,' she said, venturing a smile and then withdrawing it instantly as she saw the chill in his eyes.

He held out a hand. 'Show me the accounts.'

Her heart lifted. There was hope, after all. Why would he want to see the accounts if he wasn't considering extending the loan? She hastily opened the case, hating the fact that her hands were shaking slightly. She was on the spot and he was trying to catch her out. *It was like being back at school again.* Back in that hideous torture chamber where everyone was just waiting for her to fail.

You're stupid, Grace Thacker. Thick. Concentrate, you brainless girl.

Taking a deep breath, she reminded herself that she wasn't in school now and that she'd come a long way since those awful days.

And she *wasn't* going to fail.

Reaching into the case, she pulled out the neat pile of papers that her father had carefully collated and handed them to him.

He flicked through the pages with lean, bronzed fingers. 'This is still your five minutes, Miss Thacker. Keep talking.'

Didn't he need a moment to concentrate?

Envying the ease with which his eyes skimmed the figures, taking them all in at a glance, she looked away and tried to forget he was there as she outlined her plans for the future. She told him about the new sites she'd found, about her plans to extend each café.

Revealed her dream.

And received no reaction from him. He picked up a pen, made a few notes, flicked over the page and then finally lifted his gaze. 'I admire you, Miss Thacker.'

From the ashes of disappointment she felt a warm glow of hope. 'You do?'

'Yes. I always admire people with nerve.' He fingered the papers in front of him and she could see the strength in his hands. 'In the circumstances I would have expected you to be hiding on the opposite side of the globe.'

Grace pressed her shaking knees together. 'Hiding?'

'I'm not a very nice person when I'm crossed.'

She had the distinct feeling that she was missing something. 'Then I won't cross you,' she said lamely, the friendly smile dying on her face under his cold gaze. 'The accounts should show you that the business has huge potential.'

'These accounts show me that you're very busy.'

'Very.'

'But not making a profit.'

She pulled a face. 'Not yet.'

'Interesting, don't you think, that you're busy and yet you're not making a profit?'

Grace stared at him. 'I suppose that's the nature of business. It sometimes takes longer than you think to get off the ground. If you look at the figures you'll see that we'll soon be in profit.'

'I'm well-acquainted with the figures, Miss Thacker.' He dropped the accounts on the table. 'And I only have one question.'

One question?

Grace straightened in her chair, feeling a wave of relief. She'd braced herself for hundreds of questions all exploring the company accounts in minute detail. And she'd been dreading it. 'Please ask your question.' She gave him a sunny smile and he watched her for a moment, his eyes fixed on her face.

'Tell me, Miss Thacker, how do you sleep at night?'

CHAPTER TWO

THE sunlight poured through the windows and Rafael Cordeiro watched as the colour fled from her cheeks.

Your game's up, beauty, he said to himself, wondering how she could have been so naïve as to think that he wouldn't discover what was going on in her company. Not that she hadn't been clever, because she had. The numbers added up. Most people wouldn't have spotted what he had.

Most people didn't have his lack of faith in human nature.

At first glance her accounts appeared to reveal nothing more than a business that was slow to get off the ground. And her apparent desire to be friendly and chatty was a strategy that might well have succeeded with a man less cynical and experienced with her sex than him. Grace Thacker came across as engaging, enthusiastic and refreshingly open.

A different man could have been impressed by her admission of disappointment that her business should have been in profit by now.

A different man might have allowed himself to believe in her innocence.

It was fortunate for him, and *unfortunate* for her, that his speciality was greedy, unscrupulous women. Had that not been the case, his suspicions wouldn't have been roused and he would never have discovered that Café Brazil wasn't what it claimed to be and that Grace Thacker was a long way from being the caring, magnanimous employer that she pretended to be.

The fact that she had the nerve to turn up here and beg him to keep pouring money into her little scam was yet another testament to her greed and lack of conscience.

In normal circumstances he would have allocated one of his staff to sort out the problem, but in Grace Thacker's case he'd decided that he was going to deal with her personally.

Looking at her polished nails and shiny hair, he felt a slow, burning anger build inside him. She looked pampered and secure and it was quite obvious that she didn't know the meaning of the word hardship. *Did she have any idea how it felt to be cold and hungry? Did she know what it felt like to try and sleep without a roof over her pretty little head?*

No, of course she didn't. Why would she?

He was willing to bet that the biggest struggle in her life so far had been deciding which heels to wear with which outfit.

When she'd contacted him, requesting a meeting, his initial reaction had been to refuse. Why waste his time on her? But then he'd decided on a different approach.

Retribution.

Grace Thacker had shattered lives and was about to shatter more.

She should be made to face the consequences of her unscrupulous behaviour. She should be made to suffer. He hadn't decided how yet, but he was working on it.

And looking at her now, dressed in a suit that had undoubtedly cost an obscene amount of money, wearing shoes that shrieked of sex, expecting him to extend his loan in her business, he knew he'd made the right decision.

Just how far, he wondered idly as he admired her slender ankles and the soft curve of her calf, was she prepared to go in her attempts to persuade him? It was a pity for her that he never allowed his sex life and his business life to overlap because the chemistry between them had been live and electric from the moment she'd caught her heel on the walkway. She'd stooped to release her shoe and that action had allowed him a tempting vision of lacy white bra and creamy cleavage. Her silky sheet of blonde hair had swung forward over her face and her lips had parted in a soft gasp as she'd struggled not to lose her balance.

For a moment the anger simmering to life inside him had been overwhelmed by a surge of masculine lust so intense that it had bordered on the painful.

And then she'd noticed him. And had clutched at her briefcase like a lifebelt. That gesture alone had been sufficient to quench his libido and remind him of the reason she was here.

Money.

Aside from the shiny hair, the tempting cleavage and the long legs, Grace Thacker was no different from any other greedy woman.

Dark memories swirled up from the recesses of his mind but he pushed them away with ruthless determination, instead turning the full force of his anger onto Grace Thacker.

No wonder her father hadn't come, he thought bitterly. They obviously hadn't wanted anything to dilute the pure, virginal image she presented in her white shirt and her clean, shiny hair. If she'd been standing in front of a judge and jury, they'd have cleared her of murder.

She stood, frozen to the spot, her expression suitably confused as she considered his question. 'Why would I have trouble sleeping at night?' Her expression was innocent, her complexion as pure and English as clotted cream.

He was willing to bet she'd had a traditional English up-bringing. She'd probably attended one of those starched girls' boarding-schools that taught the essential rule for surviving in life—namely how to part a man from his wallet.

The usual technique was to marry a rich guy and then divorce and take him to the cleaners. The three Rs of female money-making—Reel in a wealthy guy, Rip him off and Retire.

He wondered why Grace Thacker hadn't taken that route. Perhaps she considered it too much bother.

He suppressed his natural inclination to confront her with the information in his possession and conclude the meeting as swiftly as possible.

That approach made it all a bit too easy for her, didn't it? She'd protest a bit at first, probably bluster and deny everything until she realised just how much he knew, then she'd probably use tears or sex to persuade him not to prosecute. Either way, she'd fly back to London without her loan and that would be the end of that.

And he didn't want it to be the end.

She was going to suffer. He wanted her to feel some of the worry and uncertainty that she'd inflicted on others. And she *was* worried, he could see it in her eyes. Despite the act, Grace Thacker was nervous.

'Why would you think I might not be able to sleep at night?' Her blue eyes were wide. 'You mean, because I'm worrying about how we'll pay off our debts if you call in your loan?'

No, he hadn't meant that, but he decided to go along with her. '*Are* you worried?'

'Of course.' She gave him a shy smile that faltered under his grim stare. 'So many people are depending on me but you just have to push that out of your head, don't you, or you'd go nuts?'

He leaned back in his chair and watched her, searching for cracks, flaws. Any sign that she had a human streak. *Any sign of remorse.* But there was nothing. Just a flicker of wariness that suggested that *he* was the one who was being unreasonable. 'So you don't think about other people?'

She frowned slightly. 'Well, it's hard not to, when you're responsible for their income, but it's important that you don't let emotion affect what needs to be done or everyone suffers.'

Memories, vile and deadly, slid into his brain and this time there was no holding them back.

Suddenly he was eight years old again. *Eight years old and totally alone. Starving hungry. Frightened. Lost in the dark. Surrounded by menacing and unfamiliar sounds that all meant danger.* Freezing sweat bathed his body and he rose to his feet and paced across to the window, struggling to free himself from the dark tentacles of his past.

For a moment he stood still, steadying his breathing, and then he turned to face her, nothing of his feelings showing on his face. 'So would you describe yourself as ruthless?'

'Honestly?' The corners of her soft mouth lifted. 'No, I'm not. But I don't think you necessarily have to be ruthless to succeed in business.'

'What about deceitful and manipulative?' Rafael kept his tone neutral. 'Are those qualities that you consider necessary for corporate advancement?'

She stared at him. 'I don't understand where this conversation is going.'

'No?' But she was wondering, she had to be.

And suddenly he decided on a course of action.

He was going to show her the consequences of her actions. Personally. And, in doing so, he was going to make sure that she suffered. *Really suffered.* His eyes rested on the neat little suit and the sexy shoes with the thin, tall heel. *Oh, yes, she was going to suffer.*

Generally speaking his interest in women's clothing was only sparked by the removal process, but he did know that four-inch heels and the jungle were a less than promising combination. 'Did you pack a bag, Miss Thacker?'

'For what?'

'I want you to stay for a few days, as my guest.' He pushed away a disturbingly clear image of her naked body reclining in his sumptuous guest bedroom and instead imagined her picking her way along a rough jungle path in a pair of heels designed for a short stroll round a glittery shopping mall. 'You've come all this way. There are a few things I'd like to show you, while you're here.'

Like snakes, spiders and more jungle than you've ever dreamed of.

The wariness in her eyes grew. 'A moment ago you were telling me that I only had ten minutes. Why would you suddenly invite me to stay?'

Because he was going to drive her tension levels into outer space. And then he was going to make her sorry. Really, really sorry.

'I'm always impressed by determination, Miss Thacker,' he drawled, suppressing the irony in his tone. 'You've earned yourself extra time.'

There was a flicker of hope in her eyes. 'You're prepared to give me more time?'

'Providing you agree to let me show you the magic of our rainforest.' His silky tone didn't appear to ring any alarm bells because she gave him a warm, trusting smile.

'Thank you so much.' She clasped her hands in front of her. 'You won't regret it. We can chat on the journey.'

Chat? Wondering whether to point out that the word didn't actually exist in his vocabulary, Rafael shot her an incredulous glance and then realised that she truly had absolutely no concept of what lay in store for her.

By the time he'd finished with her she was more likely to be screaming than chatting.

'I look forward to showing you some of the rare and beautiful sights of my country,' he purred. 'I would relish the opportunity to take you to certain parts which I think would be of interest.'

One of which might well be his bedroom, he thought idly, watching the colour that touched her cheeks. It was true that he preferred to keep his business life and his sex life separate, but Grace Thacker couldn't really be counted as business because he was going to see to it personally that her business was finished. Which meant that he could legitimately turn his attention to pleasure.

'I hadn't planned on sightseeing.'

'I'm talking about visiting the *fazenda.* The coffee farm that supplies your chain. It's right that you should know more about the product you sell.' He watched her carefully but she simply smiled and the smile put dimples in her cheeks and made her seem even younger.

'I couldn't agree more. I'd love to visit the coffee growers. My father insisted on doing that bit when we originally set up the deal. What a great idea.'

Ignoring the dimples and the sudden heat in his loins, Rafael suddenly wanted to laugh.

For sheer bald front, you couldn't fault her. By now she had to be wondering just how much he knew about her and yet there wasn't even a flicker of guilt in her eyes. Or concern about his proposal to take her deep into the jungle. She just stood there in her perfectly cut Armani suit, balancing on four-inch heels, as if tramping through the Brazilian rainforest was something she'd packed for and which she frequently did in her spare time.

She clearly had no idea what it took to walk through the jungle in the heat and humidity.

Five minutes, he said to himself with grim satisfaction. Five minutes was all it was going to take to have her shrieking about snakes and insects and clinging to him.

Without the heels, the suit and the lip-gloss she'd be lost and vulnerable.

And she'd turn to him.

And then he'd move in for the kill.

'Then I will arrange it for tomorrow.' He rose to his feet. 'In the meantime one of the staff will escort you to a room so that you can change into something more comfortable.'

'Staff?'

'Of course, staff.' He raised an eyebrow in mockery. 'You thought this was a one-man band? You think I swing through the trees in a loincloth and eat pineapples?'

'Pineapples don't grow in the Atlantic rainforest.'

She knew that much, then. Which was more than the previous female he'd brought here, who had clearly been painting her nails through all her geography lessons.

'I keep a team of staff in all my houses. It makes my working life more efficient. Your bag has already been taken up. I'll see you at dinner. Maria will prepare some local delicacies.' He waited for her shiver of apprehension but she merely smiled.

'Delicious. Thank you. You're very kind.'

Kind?

Over the years women had called him many things but never that. Rafael searched her face for irony but saw nothing except a frank, ingenuous smile.

The smile raked at his nerves. If she was worried then she wasn't letting it show and suddenly he was even more determined to put a serious dent in her composure.

By the time he'd finished with her, she wouldn't be smiling. She'd be wet and uncomfortable, her feet would be blistered, her skin covered in insect bites and she'd think twice before she ripped anyone off again.

But if she played her cards right, he just might be prepared to offer some physical consolation.

Satisfied that he was well in control of the situation, he turned his attention back to the string of phone calls that were awaiting him.

Feeling slightly shaky after her meeting, Grace followed Maria, the housekeeper, up the winding wooden stairs to her bedroom. She didn't know whether to be relieved that her ten-minute deadline had been extended or worried that she'd be spending more time in the company of Rafael Cordeiro.

She'd expected him to be tough and ruthless. After all, that was his reputation, wasn't it? It was just that she hadn't expected him to be quite so cold and intimidating.

But it was probably her fault, she thought gloomily. After all, there was no arguing that her company accounts were less than impressive. And he wasn't a man who made allowances for naïvety and inexperience. He wasn't a man who made allowances for *anything*.

Grace glanced upwards, wondering how far up the staircase went. To her right were windows, offering tempting views of the forest from different heights, to her left a carved wooden handrail. They seemed to be climbing up to the sky.

At least more time would help her plead her case, she thought as she walked upwards. She'd have a chance to elaborate on all her plans for the business. Given time, she was sure that she could show him that, whatever she lacked in experience, she made up for with sheer determination and hard work.

She'd been expecting ten minutes in which to present her case and now it seemed that she'd have considerably longer.

She should be happy, shouldn't she? Not nervous.

Wondering why he'd suddenly changed his mind, she suddenly realised that they'd reached the top of the staircase. It opened straight into a large room, two sides of which were open to the forest.

Realising that they were level with the treetops, Grace walked across to the carved wooden balcony, which prevented any occupants of the room plunging down to the forest floor. Thoroughly enchanted, she turned to the housekeeper with a smile. 'It's really beautiful. Like being in a tree-house.'

A seven-star tree-house.

Even though it had been designed to blend in with nature and provide an enviable peep into the mysteries of the rainforest, no luxury had been spared. The room was dominated by a large bed with an intricately carved headboard that demanded closer scrutiny. The cream silk sheets were topped with a velvety throw and softened by piles of cushions in myriad shades of green, which blended with the trees around. A large woven rug almost covered the wooden floor and a gentle breeze played with the filmy gauze curtains that hung in the corners of the room, more for decoration than utility.

The woman said something in a language that Grace assumed to be Portuguese and she gave an apologetic smile, feeling thoroughly embarrassed. 'I'm so sorry, I don't speak a word of Portuguese.'

'I said that your clothes have already been unpacked. If you need anything else, you only have to ask.' Her voice was soft, her English heavily accented, and Grace nodded.

'Thank you.' She cast a rueful glance down at herself. 'I'm going to change.' She felt sticky and uncomfortable and desperate to get out of her clothes. Not that she'd brought much with her. She'd packed for two nights in Rio de Janeiro. Just long enough for her to fly out to Forest Lodge and back before catching her return flight to London.

It hadn't entered her head that he'd invite her to remain as his guest in the rainforest.

She felt a burst of optimism. Wasn't this what she'd hoped

for? More time in which to persuade him to extend the loan? Well, now she had that time.

'Dinner is served in two hours, on the terrace. If you would like to swim then you can use the forest pool. Take the path on your right and walk for about five minutes. When it forks, go right again.' Maria gave her an uncertain smile. 'If you need anything else, please call me.'

Thinking that all she really needed was an extra dose of courage to go another round with Rafael Cordeiro, Grace smiled. 'I'm sure I'll be fine. Thank you.'

Deciding that the privacy of her bedroom was preferable to a pool that might have other occupants, Grace chose to ignore the offer of a swim.

Relieved to be able to strip off the suit, she showered and washed her hair. Fortunately the potential problem of what to wear for dinner was instantly solved by the fact that, apart from a red swimming costume packed in case there was a chance to swim in the hotel pool, she only had three items at her disposal. The scratchy formal suit, which she'd taken off with a sigh of relief, the combat trousers she'd worn for the long plane journey from London to Rio and a simple linen dress, packed to give her something to wear around the hotel in Rio. Three outfits and three pairs of shoes. Remembering his comments about sex, she immediately dismissed the idea of wearing her heels. Obviously the lightweight hiking boots that she'd worn on the plane were completely unsuitable, which just left the flat ballet pumps.

Reminding herself that she wasn't dressing to impress the billionaire Brazilian, she slipped her feet into the pumps and reached for the dress.

It felt wonderfully comfortable after the heavy suit and by the time she walked through the main glass atrium of Forest Lodge and onto the shaded terrace, her confidence was slightly restored. She'd cooled down and had time to think about the situation.

Everything would be fine. She simply had to let him see her passion for the business. If he saw just how much she was prepared to give, then he'd extend the loan.

Her confidence lasted as long as it took her to join him at the table.

He'd changed into a dark shirt and a pair of lightweight trousers. In the fading evening light he looked masculine, sexy and totally unnerving.

'Sit down. Drink? *Caipirinha?*'

She looked at the fresh, exotic-looking cocktail he was drinking. 'I'd better not.' She smiled at Maria, who was hovering. 'Something non-alcoholic? Juice would be lovely.'

Rafael gave a faint smile. 'Keeping your wits about you?'

Grace waited until the drink was in front of her and they were alone before she replied. 'You're very angry with me, aren't you?' *Hating* tense atmospheres, she decided on the direct approach. 'I know I've made mistakes but everyone does when they start in business.'

'Do they?' He was relaxed and in control, his handsome features displaying not a flicker of emotion, and she watched with a growing feeling of helplessness.

How did you communicate with someone like him? Someone who lived his life through facts and numbers? *Did he really feel nothing?* And then she remembered his acrimonious divorce and knew that the man *had* to have scars. When life attacked you, it left wounds. She knew that. Is that what had happened with him? Had he learned to bear his scars and keep on walking? Had his wife's abrupt departure stopped him feeling or had that happened long before his marriage had ended?

'You've never made a mistake, Mr Cordeiro?'

His mouth twisted into a cynical smile and everything about his face was suddenly brutally hard—his aggressive jaw, the glint in his eyes and the set of his shoulders. 'Yes.'

Grace looked at him closely, wondering.

He'd spoken just one word and yet why did she have the feeling that the brevity of his response concealed a weight of suffering? Why did she feel that, when there was nothing about this man that suggested weakness or vulnerability? She sensed him wrestling with something deep and dark. Something he refused to surrender to. Because this man would never surrender, she knew that. He was a bare-knuckle fighter.

'Well, I made mistakes, I admit that—' she broke off and hesitated, finding it difficult to voice the truth '—I was foolish. Naïve. Inexperienced. Call it what you like.'

He studied her for a long moment. 'Naïve, foolish and inexperienced. Are those words you're using supposed to describe yourself?'

'If I did that then there'd be no chance that you'd carry on lending me the money,' she said lightly, her eyes drawn to the strength of his forearms. 'But they're a fair description of the way I was five years ago when you first gave me the loan.'

'How old were you?'

'Eighteen. Fresh out of school.' She said the word lightly, careful to betray nothing of the misery of her school days.

'Why didn't you go to university?'

All sorts of reasons.

Grace dropped her eyes to her plate, seeing the food for the first time. When had that arrived? It occurred to her with an uncomfortable jolt that when she was with him she didn't actually notice anything but the man. 'University wasn't for me.' Her heart rate increased as they grazed over a topic that she hated. 'I wanted to set up the business.' *She'd needed to prove herself.*

His fingers played with the stem of his wine glass. 'You mean you wanted to start making money.'

Money? Grace frowned. She wanted to tell him that it wasn't about the money. Even now, she hardly took much of a salary, choosing instead to plough her share back into the business. For her, it had never been about the money, but that sort of honest admission was unlikely to get her far with a man whose driving force was financial gain. 'I wanted something that was mine,' she said finally, allowing him a small slice of the truth.

He paused as Maria added more bowls of food to the table. 'But the business was your father's.'

She shook her head. 'Not the cafés. He was importing the coffee and selling it on, but the cafés were my idea. When I left school I worked in a café for a while and I enjoyed it but there were so many things I would have done differently. I had friends at university in London who had nowhere nice to meet up during the day and that's when I had the idea of setting up on my own. I did some research, found a run-down café that was in receivership and I bought it with a loan from the bank. I spent day and night doing it up myself because I didn't have enough money to pay anyone else to help.' She reached forward and helped herself to some food. 'There were cracks in the walls that paint wouldn't cover so I decided to cover them with huge photographs of the rainforest. The effect was amazing. Everyone used to come in and ask "where's that?" I probably could have started up a second business as a travel agent.' Things had seemed so uncomplicated then. She'd started off with just one objective—*to impress her father.*

'Brazil is a beautiful country.'

'Yes. And the photos made me think about the whole experience I wanted to offer. It's quite a crowded market but most of the coffee shops in existence were targeting young mothers with children and businessmen dashing in for a quick shot of caffeine.' She picked up her fork and frowned. 'I wanted to create a place where students could meet up with their friends and enjoy conversation and fantastic music in a lively environment. The atmosphere was young and vibrant. We played samba music, sold Brazilian snacks. We had internet points so that the students could work while they drank their coffee.'

'And it was a success.'

'Yes. The place was packed and our profit was amazing. It was incredibly exciting.'

'Making money always is.'

Roused out of her memories by his slightly abrasive tone, she glanced at him, wondering if there was something more behind his comment, but his handsome face revealed nothing of his thoughts. Was she being over-sensitive? 'Yes, well, that's when I decided that we could do the same thing in other places. The bank wouldn't lend me any more money because I was so inexperienced and they didn't want to give too much money to an eighteen-year-old, which was when I approached your company. Because you were offering business loans to initiatives that supported Brazilian enterprise, I thought you might help us.' And the loan his company had given her had changed her life.

He reached for his wine glass. 'Your first café made you a profit, no?'

'Yes.'

'But now you are not in profit.' His tone was conversational. 'That must be very—disappointing.'

'We spent too much on the refurbishment.' Grace watched as he drank, unconsciously following the movement of his throat with her eyes. 'I paid a building company to do what I did myself in the first café. They cost more than I'd budgeted. It was a mistake but it isn't one I'll make again.'

'No.' His gaze lingered on her face. 'You won't.'

The tension in the atmosphere overwhelmed her and she put her fork down. 'You're going to say no, aren't you? And it's just because I haven't increased your investment yet.' Emotion bubbled up inside her. 'I haven't *lost* your money, either. You haven't *lost* anything. You're a billionaire—this investment is nothing to you. But it's everything to me and the people who work for me.' She pushed her plate away, suddenly feeling too sick to even contemplate eating. 'Why invite me to stay and visit the coffee farm if you're just going to say no?'

He didn't smile. 'You still have time to change my mind, Miss Thacker. And I know that the family who own the *fazenda* would like to meet you and hear what you have to say.'

'Hear what I have to say about what?'

She stared at him, her expression blank and uncomprehending. He made it sound as though she were going to stand up and give evidence.

'Your business, Miss Thacker. As they are your sole supplier, your business is their business. Your fortunes are inextricably linked.'

'That's true.'

This man held her future in his hands and at that moment the future looked precarious. She should have been using every last ounce of brainpower to try and understand him so that she could find ways to change his mind.

And yet she was finding it almost impossible to concentrate. Instead of being crisp and businesslike, all she could do was notice tiny irrelevant details. Like the tangle of dark chest hair just visible at the open neck of his shirt, the movement of his hands—decisive and confident. And then there was his mouth. There was something about the sensual lines of his mouth that constantly drew her attention—something wholly masculine that hinted at an extremely physical nature. Grace suddenly remembered the pilot telling her that women flocked around him.

At the time she'd dismissed his assessment as a natural consequence of wealth and power, but now she realised that it was something else entirely, something to do with the very essence of the man.

Rafael Cordeiro was full-blooded Brazilian male. He

throbbed with concentrated, full-on sex appeal and masculine supremacy. If he'd been penniless, women would still have flocked. And sharing the same space as him made her immediately aware of their differences.

Aware of her femininity.

She was so mesmerised by him that it was only when a cup of coffee was put in front of her that she realised that her plate had been discreetly removed.

Forcing herself to concentrate on something other than him, she lifted the cup to her lips, sniffed and gave an appreciative sigh. No matter what the stresses, coffee always soothed her. 'That has to be the best smell in the world.'

'I'm glad you think so. That coffee comes from the local *fazenda* that supplies your business.'

She sipped. 'It's delicious.' Perhaps the owners of the *fazenda* would add their plea to hers because if her business closed down then they'd have to find a new buyer for their coffee. 'I'm really looking forward to my visit.'

'Good.'

'Well—' she placed the cup back down on the table '—we seem to have spent the entire evening talking about me, which is very boring. What about you? Were you born and bred in Brazil?'

'I don't understand what possible relevance my heritage can have on the survival of your business,' he said softly, his accent strangely thickened. 'Take my advice and concentrate on the things that matter.'

'I just wondered about you, that's all.'

'I never talk about myself. Remember that.' He rose to his feet in a lithe movement and she had the distinct impression that her simple question had troubled and unsettled him.

'Why? Because if I find something out you'd have to kill me and then eat me?' She made the joke in a pathetic attempt to raise a smile from him but there was nothing in his face that wasn't bleak, dark and cynical and Grace allowed her own smile to die. 'I'm not a journalist or a gossip, Mr Cordeiro. And I don't think any of the tabloid newspapers would be interested in my visit to your lodge.'

His powerful body was taut, as if she was treading on a subject that he loathed. 'Be ready early, wear something that dries easily because this is a rainforest and you're likely to get wet. Extremely wet.'

'No four-inch heels, then.' Noting the forbidding, rigid lines of his mouth, she sighed.

His body language was stating clearly that nothing had changed between them, despite the fact that they'd spent an evening in one another's company. There was no softening and no reassurance.

She might have been given an extension on the ten minutes but it was clear that she wasn't expected to interpret the gesture as encouragement.

But if he had no intention of extending her loan, why bother taking her to see the *fazenda?*

Looking at the grim set of his lean, handsome face, she felt her insides lurch. She didn't know what was going on in his mind but she was willing to bet that it was nothing good or gentle.

Wound up by the conversation, Grace slept badly and all around her the rainforest intruded. It was alive with sounds, squawks, howls, chirps and the occasional growl that made her wish there was glass between her and the treetops. And when she did doze, she slept lightly, her head full of images of an arrogant Brazilian billionaire with a tormented past and a dark, controlling personality.

At one point she gave up on sleep and wandered over to the window, discovering that it overlooked the smooth glass dome that housed his office. *And he was there.* Even in the darkness of the night he was at his computer, the phone trapped between his cheek and his shoulder, eyes fixed on the screen. He sprawled in the chair, the sleeves of his now rumpled shirt pushed up past the elbows and his jaw dark with stubble.

So being in the rainforest didn't stop him working, then? Didn't stop him steering his slick, impressive corporation to still more dizzying heights.

He might be hidden away in the jungle but he was still well and truly connected to civilisation.

Why couldn't he sleep?

What was the cause of the hardness she saw in his eyes?

The questions mounted as she stood there watching and then finally she withdrew, feeling as though she was intruding on a private part of his life. After all, if he didn't choose to go to bed and rest, that wasn't her business, was it?

He wasn't exactly the sort of man who would welcome the offer of a listening ear.

She slid back into bed, pushing aside images of glossy black hair and an arrogant male profile.

When she finally woke from the fitful doze that had replaced sleep, it was raining. A steady downpour soaked the trees outside her room and dampened the sounds but the air was still muggy and oppressively warm.

Wondering whether one ever became accustomed to the suffocating heat, she dressed in her light combat trousers and a simple white shirt, slipped her feet into her hiking boots and tied her hair back.

What would he say, she wondered, *if he knew that she was far more comfortable in the boots and trousers than she'd been in the suit and heels?*

He probably wouldn't believe her. Clearly he had strongly felt prejudices about women. Where had they come from? And would his unfavourable judgement of her sex reflect on her?

Determined to think positive, she stared into the mirror and gave herself a pep talk.

It was a new day. Yesterday was gone and she had this one, whole day in which to change his mind about extending her loan.

One more day to persuade him that maintaining his investment in her business was a good thing for everyone. Although why he was so concerned about what must be for him a minuscule amount of money, she didn't understand.

Was it really all about money for him? Or was there something else lurking in those dark, brooding shadows? Something that he didn't share with strangers.

Something that kept him awake deep into the night.

He was talking on the phone again when Maria showed her into his office and she stood in tense, salient anticipation as he concluded what was obviously a business conversation. He spoke in short, clipped tones, delivering orders in an authoritative style that made her feel sorry for the person on the other end of the phone.

Did anyone like working with him? Or did they all spend their lives in a state of nervous tension?

When she had meetings with her team they slipped off their shoes and curled up on sofas with mugs of tea. Everyone gave their opinion and argued loudly.

She gave a wry smile.

But her business wasn't exactly thriving, was it?

Perhaps she ought to go to her room and practise developing a more autocratic style.

He ended the call and looked at her. 'What—no suit? No heels?'

He obviously thought she was some sort of fashion clotheshorse and his comment confirmed her suspicion that he was probably used to women who shopped and never dropped. She decided to keep the conversation businesslike. 'You told me to dress for the jungle. When does the helicopter arrive?'

'We're not using the helicopter, Grace.' His voice was silky smooth. 'We're walking. I hope those boots of yours aren't for show because you're about to be tested.'

Was that supposed to frighten her? She almost laughed. What he didn't know was that her whole life had been spent being tested. *Why,* she wondered, *did everyone in the world always expect her to fail?* Making a mental note not to utter a single word of complaint, she lifted her chin. 'Fine. Test away. If you're waiting for me to collapse then you're going to be waiting a long time.'

'Good, because I have no desire to scrape you off the jungle floor or drag you from the coils of an anaconda.'

'What is your problem?' She looked at him in genuine bewilderment. 'You want me to fail, don't you? You want me to make a fool of myself. Why? Just because my company hasn't made you enough money? Is it really that important?'

He studied her for a moment and then bent and retrieved two rucksacks from the floor. 'It's a two-hour walk, providing the rain doesn't cover the path.' He thrust a rucksack into her hands. 'Let's go. We'll eat breakfast on the way.'

He hadn't answered her question but she was left with a horrible sinking feeling that she was going to discover the answer soon enough.

CHAPTER THREE

THE RAIN FELL STEADILY and Rafael trudged up the path, occasionally casting a glance over his shoulder to check that Grace was with him. A reluctant smile touched his mouth as he saw her plodding behind him, her blonde hair now soaked and sleek against her head, the rain turning it from bright summer wheat to rich, old gold. Her clothes were saturated and clung to her body, revealing every line and contour of her slender frame.

Slender but with curves in *all* the right places.

He should have put her in front, he thought idly, so that he could at least have admired the view while they walked.

Instead of which, she was the one looking at him. Occasionally he intercepted a curious glance, as if she couldn't quite work out what he had planned for her. As if she couldn't work *him* out and he found her frank, appraising stare profoundly irritating.

And he was feeling something else as well. Something a thousand times more powerful than curiosity or irritation.

Chemistry. Electric, fiery chemistry that snapped the air taut and made his body throb in a vicious response that was entirely sexual.

Which all went to prove that the male libido was no judge of character, a fact that he'd learned a long time before.

With a shake of his head and a cynical smile, he continued to walk, relying on hard physical exercise to dampen the almost painful reaction of his body.

And to her credit, at least she wasn't a moaner. So far he hadn't heard a single comment about blisters or broken nails, wet hair or insect bites. He'd expected her to crack or at least show signs of nerves or exhaustion but she just kept on going, planting her feet firmly in front of her. And on the few occasions when she'd slipped on the increasingly muddy path, she'd regained her balance and glared at him, as if daring him to patronise her with an offer of help that they both knew would be delivered with condescension.

Even when they'd had to cross the river and she'd slipped on the glassy boulders and fallen neck-deep in the water, she'd ignored his outstretched hand. Instead she'd dragged herself bodily over the rocks until she'd reached the other side. Watching her brush an insect away from her neck with an impatient flick of her hand, he suddenly had a strong feeling that her performance was driven by something far stronger, deeper and more powerful than a reaction to his comment about her suit and high heels. Something that came from deep inside her.

What was she trying to prove? And to whom?

He already knew everything that he needed to know about her.

All the figures pointed to the fact that she was a liar, a cheat and a fraud.

So why did he keep turning his head to glance at her?

Why was he so fiercely aware of her?

She was bedraggled, messy and horribly uncomfortable, but still she walked. Occasionally she paused to squint into the trees but it wasn't fear he saw in her eyes, but interest.

'What's that?'

He paused and followed her gaze, looking through the tangled vines wrapped around tall, dignified trees that stood straight as soldiers. 'What?'

'Up there.' She brushed damp hair out of her eyes and pointed. 'That red bird. It's beautiful.'

He studied her face, wondering if this was all part of her act. But her blue eyes were fixed on the blur of red feathers in the branches above and when she turned to him there was a smile on her mouth.

'You don't know, do you?' Her eyes teased and mocked as she adjusted the rucksack on her back. 'This is virtually your back garden and you can't name it.'

'This isn't a nature tour,' he said roughly, glancing up as a crack of thunder splintered the air above them and the rain intensified. 'We'll shelter for a moment.'

He pulled her under the shelter of the nearest tree and she pushed her soaking hair away from her face, her eyes gleaming with laughter, and he had a powerful feeling that she was actually enjoying herself.

'What's the point in sheltering?' Drops of water clung to her lashes and spilled down her cheeks like tears. 'Once you've fallen in the river, you can't get any wetter. I've reached saturation point.' As if to prove it, she twisted the edges of her shirt between her hands and chuckled as the water dripped to the ground. 'See what I mean?'

They'd been walking for over an hour. She had to be tired but she hadn't once complained and Rafael felt a flicker of reluctant admiration. Greedy and deceitful she undoubtedly was, but you had to give her credit for being tough. Offhand, he didn't know another woman who would have cheerfully discarded their high heels in favour of boots and then coped with the rainforest without a word of complaint.

But she didn't dare complain, he reminded himself, determinedly reining in the almost vicious reaction of his body. She was still hoping that she could talk him out of his money.

Angry with his own response, Rafael turned to look down

the path but in only a matter of seconds his gaze was drawn back to the girl.

What was it about her?

What was it about her that stirred him, even though she had absolutely no qualities that he admired? What did she have, this golden-haired English girl who was so lacking in morals?

She was leaning with her back against the tree. Her eyes had drifted shut as she breathed in the scent of the rainforest and there was something almost shockingly sensual about her transformation from city girl to forest dryad. Her flushed cheeks were damp and drops of water clung to the soft curve of her mouth and she seemed to blend with the nature that surrounded her. It was as if she were part of the forest, put there to tempt man.

And tempt she did.

Hot waves of lust engulfed him as he dragged his eyes away from her mouth and allowed his gaze to travel lower.

The rain had rendered her white shirt virtually see-through and he was given a tempting view of firm, high breasts and nipples clearly defined as they strained against the wet fabric. The heat inside him grew and his eyes slid lower still, past her narrow waist and down to the point at which her trousers settled on the wholly feminine curve of her hips. Her trousers were muddy and there was a tear in one of the legs, her boots were battered, but he couldn't ever remember being so hot for a woman.

Something dangerous stirred inside him and he stood for a moment, in the grip of a lust so powerful and basic that it bordered on the primitive.

All around them were sounds of the forest and falling rain but here, in the shelter of the tree, it was just the two of them.

And perhaps she felt his gaze because her eyes opened slowly and she looked at him. Wariness gave way to curiosity and then to something else entirely—something that they both felt and shared.

For a long moment, neither of them spoke.

The air heated and crackled and that same chemistry that had been present from their first meeting sparked into life, sizzling the air like a high-voltage cable.

His resolve to wait until their business was concluded before shifting their relationship on to a more intimate level evaporated in a flash of primal heat.

Acting on the most basic of instincts, Rafael stepped forward and brought his mouth down on hers. The sexual connection was instant and he met her gasp of shock with the demands of his mouth. His body pressed her back against the rough bark of the tree and he felt her lips part under the pressure of his. She made a strange sound in her throat and then her arms were around his neck, clasping, holding on.

His hands were on her hips, on that narrow band of flesh that bridged the gap between her trousers and her shirt. Her clothes were damp but he could feel the heat of her flesh burning against his as he stroked a hand over her narrow waist and then lifted it upwards to find her breast.

Through the wet fabric he felt the hard jut of her nipple against his seeking fingers and felt her body shiver in a response that matched the intensity of his. Impatient to be closer still, he slid his fingers inside the flimsy fabric and touched warm, silky skin.

The heat between them reached flashpoint and she cried out, her mouth leaving his for a moment as her body strained closer. And then her lips were under his again and her hands moved to his chest, her fingers sliding and fumbling as she wrenched at the buttons on his shirt, parted the soaking fabric and touched him properly for the first time.

Sounds of rain and jungle life enveloped them but he heard nothing but her soft gasps and his own rough breathing as they kissed, creating magic that isolated them from their surroundings.

His tongue explored the intimate secrets of her mouth and

Rafael dropped his hands to the zip of her trousers, ready and prepared to strip her naked. Sexual hunger flared through his body, but just when he thought he might explode with the sheer intensity of that primitive urge, her hands closed over his.

'No.' The word was barely audible as her mouth slid from his and she paused for a moment as if seeking both the breath and energy to speak. 'No. We can't. We have to stop.'

Dizzy with lust and devoured by a hormonal drive for immediate satisfaction, Rafael took a moment to comply with her request. Then he stepped back, slightly shaken by the ferocity of his own response and even more surprised by her apparent desire to stop.

Why would she want to stop?

His entire body aching, Rafael glanced over his shoulder towards the path which had all but disappeared under the torrential rain. 'Trust me, no one is going to walk past, if that's what's worrying you.'

'It's not about anyone else. It's about us.'

'Us?' The word had intimate connotations that chilled him to the bone and dampened his libido more effectively than any rainstorm. 'There is no *us*.'

She brushed her hair out of her eyes with a shaking hand. 'A moment ago you were kissing me and your hands were—everywhere.'

'And?' He stared at her blankly and she shook her head.

'Well—if you kiss someone, it generally means that there's something between you.'

The air around them throbbed with the heat that they'd created and he jabbed his fingers through his hair to stop him reaching for her again. 'There's chemistry. That's what's between us.'

'But why did you kiss me?'

Because he'd wanted to? Because his body throbbed and ached every time he looked at her?

Despite his experience with women, Rafael surveyed her with something approaching incredulity. How was she managing to turn elemental sex into a conversation topic? He spread his hands in a gesture of mounting exasperation, trying to rein in the ferocious surge of animal lust that still threatened to engulf him. 'Isn't it obvious? I find you sexy.'

She tilted her head back and fastened him with her gaze. 'But you don't like me, do you?'

Rafael clenched his jaw. Never, if he lived a million years, would he understand a woman's drive to question the blindingly obvious. 'And how is that relevant?'

'I can't believe you just asked me that.' She rubbed a hand over her face to remove the raindrops that still clung. 'You were kissing me.'

'And you were kissing me back.'

'Yes.' She met his gaze without flinching. 'But then I stopped you. I can't have a relationship with someone who doesn't like me. It doesn't feel right.'

Remembering the heat of her mouth against his, Rafael was about to assure her that it had felt perfectly right, but thought better of it. 'I wasn't offering a relationship.'

'But you would have made love to me.'

His laugh held no trace of humour. *Love?* Sooner or later that word had to raise its ugly head and its appearance effectively dampened his libido and cleared the red mist from his brain. 'It was *love* that made you strip off my shirt?'

The colour poured into her cheeks. 'I admit I was—it was— I'd never felt anything like that before.' She moved away from him, as if she didn't trust herself to stand close to him and not touch him. 'But there are lots of reasons why it isn't a good idea. One of which is, like it or not, that you are responsible for my loan. It wouldn't be right.'

'You want me to guarantee your loan before we have sex?'

Well, of course she did. Furious with himself for breaking his rule and complicating the situation, Rafael felt his mouth tighten, but she shook her head.

'Of course not. I want you to extend my loan, yes, but not because of—of—anything else that happens to be between us. But if anything *did* happen then it's inevitable that you'd question my reasons for sleeping with you.'

No, he wouldn't. He'd sleep with her and forget her. Because that was the way he chose to live his life. He'd long since abandoned self-delusion. 'I'm not into analysis. When you sleep with me, I can guarantee you that there won't be post-mortem.' He ran a hand over his face to clear the water from his vision. 'Frankly, I don't care if we don't talk at all.'

Her lips parted. 'Oh, well, that's romantic.'

He leaned forward and planted an arm against the tree, bringing his body close to hers again. 'It wasn't supposed to be romantic.' He lifted her chin, forcing her to meet his gaze. 'Romantic is the lies people tell to soften the fall into bed. And I don't tell lies. Is that what you're going to do, Grace? Are you going to tell all the lies that women always tell? Because if you are, then this is the moment that you share with me that you love me. And we both know that you don't. That's not what this is about. This is about physical chemistry. The sort you don't think about.'

Something flickered in her blue eyes. 'You're very confusing.'

'No.' The irony of her statement brought a smile to his lips. 'I'm very straightforward. It's everyone around me who plays the games, Miss Thacker.'

Her chin lifted. 'I'm not playing games, but I don't sleep with men I don't know. And especially not with men who are careless about emotions.'

'I'm not careless. Not at all.' *He took great care.* He played by one set of rules. His own. And he'd made them for a reason. 'Sex is sex. It doesn't have to be complicated.'

She stared at him. 'You're telling me that you'd make love to me on the forest floor today, and then withdraw my loan tomorrow?'

'Love?' Just saying the word brought a bad taste to his mouth. 'Not love. I didn't say anything about love.'

Something flickered in her eyes. 'Emotionless sex, then.'

'Sex…' He stepped closer to her and felt the chemistry spark again like a live thing. 'It's an appetite, like hunger or thirst. An urge to be satisfied.'

'You don't truly mean that.' She made a distressed sound and paced back towards the path, rubbing her damp arms with her hands. 'I've been giving you the benefit of the doubt. I told myself that you couldn't possibly be as cold as everyone said you were. That you've had a hard time in your life and that's bound to make things difficult.'

Rafael ground his teeth with frustration. *Why did women always do that?*

Why did they always try and dissect every situation down to the bone?

'If there's one thing that dampens my libido more than a liar, it's an amateur psychologist,' he said, swinging the rucksack onto his back and striding past her onto the path. 'Sex is sex, *minha paixao,* it's just that very few women have the courage to acknowledge that fact. They prefer to dress it up in woolly emotion, bind a man with commitment and then whine when the appetite is satisfied and the whole thing falls apart. Which is why the divorce rate remains high.'

Now who was dissecting things down to the bone? Aggravated with her for driving him on to topics he made a point of avoiding and astonished with himself for not cutting her dead earlier in the conversation, Rafael tightened his mouth and started up the path.

'Is that what happened to you?' Her voice came from behind him and he turned, a growl of frustration bursting from his throat.

'*What* did you say?'

She was standing on the rain-soaked path, her blue eyes bright and intent on his, no trace of a smile on her face, and her simple, straightforward scrutiny disturbed him more than he could have imagined possible.

Without understanding why, Rafael strode back to her, the anger mounting inside him, although whether that anger was directed at himself or the girl he couldn't be sure.

All he knew was that he'd had enough of the conversation. And he'd had enough of Grace Thacker. From now on he was going to block out her curves, her dimples and her sleek, silky blonde hair because some women were just too much effort and she was one of those.

And now she was looking at him in the way women did when they wanted you to open up and spill all sorts of deep, innermost secrets that they could sell to the papers for an indecent amount of money.

Rafael almost laughed. *What would she say,* he wondered, *if she knew that the truth about him could have been sold for a small fortune?*

'I asked,' she said slowly, 'whether that was what happened to you. There has to be some reason why you feel and behave the way you do.'

He swallowed a bitter laugh. *Oh, there was.*

But what would a woman like Grace Thacker do with the information? No doubt use it to secure the loan she needed to continue with her corrupt little business.

Suddenly transported back to his childhood, he glanced around the forest but it held no fears for him now. No dark memories. In fact, it had been his sanctuary. He'd made it that way.

'Why do I behave the way I do? Because I'm a man, and that's the way men think.' Infuriated by her determination to suck information out of him, Rafael couldn't keep the impatience out of his voice and heard her sharp intake of breath.

'I just can't believe that you're as cold and insensitive as they say you are.'

'Well, I am.' His tone simmered with raw aggression as a black rage descended on him. 'Remember that before you ask personal questions that I have no intention of answering.'

Wondering what had possessed him to consider walking through the rainforest with Grace for company, Rafael ground his teeth and turned away from her but not before he saw the silent question in her eyes.

Women, he thought as he strode up the ancient path at a punishing pace.

The sooner they reached the *fazenda,* the sooner he could expose the game she'd been playing and end this farce.

And then he'd send her home.

Grace walked in silence, keeping her eyes on the path so that she didn't miss her step in the rough, slippery terrain.

But her mind wasn't on the physical challenge that the rainforest presented. *It was on the kiss—that amazing, astonishing kiss that had awakened her previously dormant body from sleep to a state of almost overwhelming excitement.* But the confusion caused by that steamy, erotic encounter in the humid, leafy jungle was eclipsed by the conversation that had followed.

And now she wished—*how desperately she wished*—that she'd kept her mouth shut.

Perhaps he was right that sex was better without conversation because words had tainted the fragile perfection of the moment.

Words—the most deadly weapon given to human beings.

She, of all people, knew the damage that words could do and

yet she'd thrown them out carelessly, with no thought to the wounds they might cause.

And now she was filled with nothing but regret and self-recrimination.

She wished she hadn't asked if he was going to extend the loan because he'd obviously interpreted her question as a signal that she'd sleep with him if he gave a positive answer.

But most of all she wished she hadn't asked the question about his marriage. It had been personal and inappropriate, she could see that now, but there had been something about his bitter remarks and the rigid tension in those broad shoulders that had made it impossible for her not to ask. *Impossible* for her not to reach out to him as she would have reached out to any human being in such intense pain.

And the pain was there, she was sure of it.

When he'd stridden back down the path towards her and the expression on his face had been so black and threatening that, for a wild, panicky moment, she'd known she'd gone too far. And she'd been afraid.

Afraid for herself.

Afraid for him.

And then she'd seen his eyes. And what she'd seen there wasn't violence but bitterness, pain and cynicism and her fear had turned back into concern and compassion.

What had caused the darkness that she so clearly saw in him?

What memories haunted his nights and kept him locked to the safe, inanimate computer screen?

And why had he kissed her?

No matter what derisive comment he made about women's attitude to sex, she wasn't so naïve and foolish that she'd interpreted their hot jungle encounter as anything other than physical lust. She knew that chemistry existed, even though she'd never experienced its explosive force before today. She understood that sex could happen without love. She understood all those things. But that didn't mean that she didn't *believe* in love.

Never having found it didn't mean that it wasn't there.

And never having found it didn't mean she didn't yearn for it.

Maybe it would never come her way, but that didn't stop her hoping because what sort of life was it without hope?

What sort of life was it without love?

And suddenly she understood the acres of dark emptiness that she'd seen in his eyes. Rafael Cordeiro was a man living a life without love.

Why?

Why had he made that choice?

And why did she even care?

CHAPTER FOUR

THEY walked without speaking, but were spared an awkward silence by the chorus of birds and frogs chirping and monkeys chattering, the now familiar rainforest sounds that provided a constant accompaniment to their physical efforts.

Occasionally Rafael glanced over his shoulder and looked at her but his gaze didn't linger and she wasn't even sure *why* he was checking on her because she had the distinct impression that he wouldn't have minded if she'd fallen head first into the river that now bubbled cheerfully alongside the path.

Clearly he was wishing himself alone in his rainforest hideaway.

She'd made the mistake of trying to reach out and touch his deep, dark secrets and, like an injured predator, he'd given her a warning.

Keep your distance.

Don't come too close.

So keep her distance she would and she wouldn't go too close.

They'd visit the *fazenda* as planned, walk back to his lodge and then he'd give her his answer about her business. And whatever that answer was, she'd leave.

And Rafael Cordeiro with his dark secrets and his cynical view of love and life would be part of her past.

Which was a good thing, she told herself as she balanced on a log and avoided a deep, muddy pool of water, because she wasn't ever going to be the sort of woman who indulged in emotionless sex and if they pursued this physical connection then that was what she'd be offered.

And emotionless sex meant giving up on a dream of something more.

And she wasn't ready to stop dreaming.

She was so wrapped up in her own thoughts that she didn't even realise that he'd stopped until she walked straight into him.

'Sorry.' Moving away from his steadying hand, she stepped back and stared into the trees. 'Why have we stopped?'

'This is the beginning of the *fazenda*.'

They were the first words he'd spoken since his response to her ill-timed question and there was no warmth. No emotion at all. Just a statement of fact. Like a tour guide, trained to impart the required information.

She glanced around herself in surprise, seeing dense jungle either side of the path. 'We're still in the rainforest.'

'The coffee is grown in the forest. The owners maintain the land around them. They run their business in perfect harmony with nature. Ecologically sound.' His mouth tightened. 'And you care about things like that, don't you, Grace?'

So they were back to that, then.

The hard glances and the sarcastic comments loaded with a meaning that she had yet to interpret. Gone was the heat and the passion that they'd shared in the pulsing heat of a rain-soaked forest. Gone was the intimacy, however shallow.

And she made no reference to it. Why would she, when she knew that what they'd shared had been fleeting and ephemeral? A transient lighting of the senses which had been quickly quenched by words, both his and hers. Something less than honest because neither *knew* the other, so how could anything built on such superficial grounds ever be deeply felt?

Moving away from such dangerous and unsettling thoughts, she played his game. 'Yes, I do care.' She refused to let his tone unsettle her. 'And I know the history of the *fazenda*. The reason we're prepared to pay the price we pay for the coffee is because it's grown in an environmentally-friendly way. If we'd used cheaper coffee then you might be seeing a return on your investment now.' And perhaps he wouldn't be so angry. It all seemed to be about money for him. Money seemed to be the only thing that mattered. And she suddenly found herself wondering about his wife, although this time she did her wondering quietly, with her mouth firmly shut.

Was that why his glamorous, high-maintenance wife had left him? Because his focus was all on dollars, cents and profit?

'You care deeply, don't you, Grace?' He was watching her and she saw the now familiar cynical gleam return to his eyes. 'I suggest we postpone this particular conversation until you've looked round the *fazenda*.'

They walked onwards past creeks and streams that had been dammed to preserve the water. Goats grazed, chickens ran loose and a group of young children were playing a riotous game in the dust outside.

As they walked towards some buildings, a man and a woman emerged to meet them. Their simple clothes were dusty from the soil and worn from years of hard use. Physical toil in the harsh Brazilian sunshine had weathered the skin on their faces and hands so that it was impossible to be sure of their age. Grace would have guessed them to be in their late sixties but they could have been younger.

Holding out both hands, the woman greeted Rafael with warmth and respect and he spoke in rapid Portuguese, his gaze occasionally sliding to Grace, leaving her in no doubt that she was the topic of conversation.

Conscious of her bedraggled appearance, Grace smoothed her hair away from her face and hoped they didn't mind the fact that she was such a mess. But they didn't seem to even notice her wet clothes. They didn't seem interested.

Instead they listened to Rafael and cast anxious glances in her direction, their smiles of welcome apparently frozen by whatever it was he was saying.

Grace sighed. Whatever it was, if the words leaving his mouth related to her, then the one thing that she could guarantee was that it wouldn't be anything flattering.

Although she didn't fully understand his animosity towards her, she could hardly fail to be aware that he wasn't exactly her biggest fan.

Except in the sex department, she reminded herself ruefully. On that level, at least, she'd apparently scored points with him.

As he talked, she sensed a change in the couple and they looked at her with a mixture of anxiety, trepidation and a touch of—anger?

Gaining the distinct impression that her unannounced arrival was less than welcome, Grace suddenly felt awkward and touched Rafael's arm. 'Does it put them out, me visiting like this? Because if it does we can just turn straight round and go home.'

'*Home?*' The mockery in his voice reminded her that, however beautiful his rainforest lodge, she had no claim on it.

She was an outsider.

And she'd never felt more alienated from others than she did at that moment.

'I mean to your lodge, of course,' she murmured, correcting her mistake swiftly and wondering why every verbal exchange between them felt like negotiating a minefield.

He studied her for a moment, his gaze direct and unsympathetic. 'Your visit doesn't put them out. But naturally it's distressing for them. And worrying.'

'Why would it be distressing? Do they know that my business is in trouble?'

But Rafael ignored her question and instead switched back to Portuguese to continue his conversation with the couple. And although she couldn't understand what he was saying, he appeared to be reassuring them about something. His reassurance appeared to have an effect because the woman reached for his hand and gave him a grateful look.

Mesmerised by the unexpected softening she saw in his dark eyes, Grace watched as his strong male fingers closed over the work-roughened hand of the old lady. Although hers wasn't the hand being squeezed, she knew instinctively that there would be pressure from those long, strong fingers and she took comfort from that surprising fact.

So he wasn't entirely incapable of emotional connection, then. Not entirely incapable of showing feeling. Not love, maybe, but something.

And not for some Hollywood 'A' list actress but for an old lady who lived in the forest. Someone whose means were quite obviously entirely different from his own.

And then he released the old lady's hand and switched back to English with an ease and fluency that Grace could only envy. Pushing aside the sense of inferiority that other people's effortless competence always induced in her, she stepped forward with a smile as he introduced them.

'Carlos and Filomena,' he said quietly. 'They farm the land along with their extended family and a few workers who come in from the nearest town.'

Grace glanced towards the children playing with the water barrel. 'Those are their children?'

'Grandchildren. Their children are out on the farm working.'

'A real family business, then.' Grace sensed a sudden stiff-ness in the couple and then Filomena stepped forward and said something in Portuguese.

'She says that they are pleased you've come here so that they have the opportunity to show you what they're doing.' There was something in his tone that made her faintly uneasy but she'd had enough of word games to last her the entire visit so she simply nodded and smiled to indicate that she was equally pleased.

They led her towards the trees, talking rapidly and waving their hands and she glanced towards Rafael for a translation, trying not to notice the way his still damp shirt clung to the width of his shoulders and the hard muscle of his torso.

'What are they saying?'

'They're telling you that the coffee is grown in shade in the forest. In that way none of the forest is destroyed and the trees fix nitrogen in the soil which helps the coffee bushes grow.' He broke off as Filomena spoke to them. 'She says that keeping the trees prevents erosion and protects the coffee from the harsh weather. The natural sugars increase and enhance the flavour of the coffee.'

'And the fallen leaves provide nutrients and help prevent moisture loss from the soil.' Grace smiled and nodded. 'Please tell them that I understand the benefits of shade-grown coffee. Every café has a wall devoted to telling that story. People enjoy their coffee knowing that they're preserving a small part of the rainforest.'

'A marketing goldmine, I'm sure.' A flicker of contempt in his eyes, Rafael studied her for a moment and then turned and spoke quietly to the woman. She responded immediately with lots of hand-waving and glances towards her husband. Voices were raised and then the woman covered her mouth with her hand and shook her head, tears welling in her eyes.

Deeply concerned, Grace stepped forward and then turned

to Rafael for a translation. 'What's wrong? What are they saying? What's going on here?'

With a determined glance towards her husband, Filomena stepped forward. *'Você toma um cafezinho?'*

Understanding that *cafezinho* was the word for coffee, Grace gave an enthusiastic nod before glancing at Rafael for confirmation. 'She's inviting me to sample the coffee?'

'She's offering you hospitality.' The sunlight gleamed on his dark head and his mouth was set in a hard line. 'In the circumstances it's more than you deserve. Accept.'

More than she deserved? 'What circumstances? Why is she upset?'

'They'd like to offer you their hospitality and in return they hope you will repay them with honesty.' His eyes shimmered with barely contained anger. 'The game is up, Miss Thacker.'

Game? What game? But she didn't have time to ask him to elaborate because he was accompanying Carlos and Filomena to the nearest house, leaving her to follow along the narrow path that traced the line of the river and then curved up a terraced slope towards the buildings that clustered against the dense, lush backdrop of the rainforest.

Drained by her abortive attempts to interpret Rafael's caustic comments, Grace glanced in surprise at the fruit trees, flowers and the wide variety of different plants. 'It's so beautiful. Do they grow other things as well as the coffee?' If she'd hoped that her interest would endear her to him then she was instantly disappointed because his reply was brief and discouraging.

'They grow a variety of crops. It's a way of minimising pests and diseases.'

'It must be hard for them, so much depending on their environment.'

They'd reached the house and Rafael stood to one side and allowed her to follow the family through, his eyes reflecting his anger. 'Not all the threats to their way of life come from the environment.'

They sat down and Grace gratefully accepted the cup of coffee she was handed. She sipped slowly and gave a low moan of appreciation as the aroma and flavour teased her senses. It was strong and sweet. 'It's delicious. It tastes even better here than it does at home.'

There was a long silence and then Filomena started to speak and there was such passion in her voice that her husband reached out and put a hand on her arm, as if trying to silence her.

Grace put her coffee-cup down on the table, suddenly aware of the atmosphere in the room. 'What's the matter?' She turned to Rafael. 'What's she saying?'

His eyes held hers. 'She wants to know why, if you like the coffee so much, you're not prepared to pay a fair price for it.'

Grace was silent for a moment as she digested his words. Was this what it was all about? He didn't think she was paying enough for the coffee? 'We pay a fair price. We sell organic, shade-grown coffee. It's part of what makes our business special. The quality of the product.'

'But quality costs, doesn't it, Grace, and it's hard to make a profit if you're paying top dollar?'

She frowned. 'You're suggesting that we don't pay a fair price for our coffee, but we pay well above the market rate. You can check the numbers.'

His gaze hardened. 'I have checked the numbers. Why do you think I refused to extend the loan I made to your company?'

'Because I hadn't made you a profit. Because...' she broke off as his words sank in. 'Are you telling me that your decision not to extend the loan was based on the price we're paying for the coffee? If that's the case then you've made a mistake. I believe in paying a good price for quality goods.'

'But to whom?'

She stared at him. 'I don't understand what you're saying.'

'Over the past few years Café Brazil has gradually squeezed the price down until this *fazenda* can barely afford to operate. Without subsidy this farm would no longer be a viable business and as it is it can no longer sustain the needs of this whole family.' His voice had an explosive edge. 'They've reached the point where the children will have to move away to try and find work. On what you pay, Carlos can't afford to feed his children and grandchildren. You're looking at the consequences of your greed, *minha paixao*. Do you understand what I'm saying now?'

Grace sat, frozen in stillness.

Greed?

As she looked at the lined, worried faces of the couple sitting in front of her, Grace's heart started banging hard against her chest. She didn't understand what she'd done wrong but it was obvious from the grim set of his features that he truly believed her guilty of a serious misdemeanour. And these people believed it too. 'We pay a great deal for the coffee,' she said hoarsely, stating one of the few things she knew to be fact. 'It's one of the reasons it's taken us so long to see a profit from the business.'

'Your company accounts would suggest otherwise.' Rafael turned his attention back to Filomena, who was speaking again. 'She says that they can no longer afford to sell to you at the price you pay. They are searching for an alternative buyer.'

'No! She mustn't do that. The coffee is really special, I know that and so do the customers. Wait a minute…' Trying to think on her feet, Grace leaned forward and stretched her hand out to the woman in a gesture of conciliation. Then she let it fall back into her lap. The woman didn't want conciliation, she wanted money and clearly she wasn't receiving it. 'Please tell her that there's been some mistake. I don't know all the facts yet but I will, I promise. I'll look into it. I'll find out what's gone wrong. But don't stop supplying us.'

'You'll look into it?' His voice was loaded with sarcasm. 'What is there to look into?'

'You've seen the accounts. You know that we pay a great deal of money for the coffee.' Her palms were sweating and she rubbed her hands over her trousers. 'It's one of the reasons that our overheads are so high.'

'I've seen that you pay a great deal of money to the dealer who imports the coffee for you.'

She stared at him. 'You're suggesting that our money isn't getting through? That the dealer my father uses is overcharging? That he's dishonest?'

He gave a faint smile. 'Oh, I don't think the dealer is the only dishonest one here. The money you're paying is grossly inflated. Far beyond the price of the coffee. I'm sure there are several beneficiaries. Unfortunately, this *fazenda* isn't one of them.'

Her mouth was suddenly dry. 'You think we have some sort of shady agreement with the importer? That he charges us too much and then we split the difference?'

'It looks that way.'

'You're accusing me of fraud.'

'That's right.' His tone was silky smooth and he seemed entirely unperturbed by her growing tension. 'I am.'

She stared at him, trying to get to grips with the enormity of his accusation. 'And it doesn't occur to you that there might be another explanation for the figures?'

'Offer me one.'

She bit her lip. 'I can't. Not yet. But I will.'

'When you've had a chance to think one up?'

'No. Not that.' She rounded on him angrily, panic pricking her usually even temper. 'When I've discovered what's been happening.'

'Perhaps you're just incredibly fond of the dealer.' His eyes dropped to her mouth and then to her breasts and his implication was obvious.

His barely veiled reference to their steamy encounter in the forest brought the colour flooding into her cheeks but she didn't respond. She opened her mouth to defend herself and then closed it again. What was the point? What was the point of telling him that she didn't normally behave with such a complete lack of restraint? It would merely flatter his already overdeveloped ego and anyway, he wouldn't believe her. And she could hardly blame him for that in the circumstances. Her response to him had been every bit as hot and uninhibited as his. 'There's obviously something going on, I agree. And I don't blame you for thinking that I'm involved because all the evidence would suggest that I am. I need to make some calls.' She muttered the words, almost talking to herself as she ran through her options. 'I need some information.'

'Don't bother with the calls. Your business is finished but you needn't worry. I'm sure you could make a reasonable living as an actress. You're very convincing.' Rafael stifled a yawn and rose to his feet. 'We need to get back to the lodge before dark. And it gets dark very quickly in the rainforest.'

She didn't care about the dark and she didn't care about the dangers lurking in the rainforest. Her demons were much closer and more real than that.

Something had gone wrong with her business. If he was right, and she had no reason to doubt him, then someone had been fiddling the books to make money.

But how could they have got away with that? And who was responsible?

She intended to find an answer to both questions just as soon as she'd persuaded Rafael Cordeiro that she was innocent.

But did it really matter what he thought of her?

What really mattered more than anything was that these people, these gentle, hospitable people, thought her guilty.

And perhaps, in a way, she *was* guilty, she thought miserably as she sifted through the sparse facts at her disposal.

True, she hadn't taken the money but it *was* her business, her accounts, and she hadn't noticed that anything was amiss.

Racked with contrition for the fact that they'd suffered because of her, she tried to work out what she could do to make amends. Impulsively she dropped to her knees and took Filomena's hand in hers.

'I will find out what's happened and I will repay the money we owe to you. Your family will not suffer,' she promised, her voice shaking with emotion. She turned her head and spoke to Rafael, her voice fierce. 'Translate for me.'

His eyes were cold. 'I don't believe in giving false hope.'

'Translate for me!' The emotion in her voice clearly had some effect because he studied her for a long moment and then gave a faint shrug and said something in Portuguese to the woman.

Filomena hesitated and then put a hand on Grace's shoulder and nodded.

'There we are,' Rafael's voice held a sharp edge, 'you've convinced her that you're as innocent as the dawn. Happy now? Is that your motto? Why let someone down once if you can let them down twice?'

Still racked by self-reproach, she stood up, her fingers biting into her palms. 'No. I'm not at all happy. I'm not happy that they've been hurt and that they're struggling because of me. And I'm not happy that someone is using my business for personal gain. This is my life you're talking about. Café Brazil means something to me. We were helping people. Helping people who were struggling.' *And she knew all about how it felt to struggle.*

'I'm sure you were.' His faint smile was derisory. 'You're just a saint, Grace Thacker. A saint in high heels.'

Her mouth tightened. 'Obviously there's something going

on and, in the circumstances, I can't blame you for thinking that I'm involved. But I'm not. And you obviously have no idea how upset I am.' What an enormous blow it was. Everything she'd built was collapsing around her and she had none of the answers. How? *How?*

For a moment she felt old familiar feelings of helplessness roll over her and she just wanted to curl up into a ball and hide from her life.

And then she looked at Filomena's craggy, anxious features and heard the children playing outside, shrieking and laughing, with no idea that their future was in jeopardy. She couldn't curl into a ball and there was no hiding.

People were relying on her.

She lifted her chin and looked him in the eye. 'I find your assumption that I had something to do with this really offensive.'

'I find fraud offensive, particularly when the victims are innocent Brazilians.'

She took a deep breath. 'Given what you've told me, you have a perfect right to be angry and I understand now why you refused to extend the loan on the business.'

'Good. Then we won't need to waste any more of each other's time.'

'Don't say that.' She reached out and put a hand on his arm, the message in her eyes suggesting that this was the most important thing that had ever happened to her. 'If you pull the loan on my business then I can't put this right. I can't fix things. And I want to.'

His gaze was blisteringly unsympathetic. 'I'm sure you do. It can't be easy to see such a large part of your income about to vanish in smoke.'

'I don't care about my income. This isn't about my money. Why can't you believe that? If something has happened then it's happened without my knowledge.'

The expression in his eyes was as hard as the tone of his voice. 'You're a director of the company and you have access to the company accounts. It would be impossible for you not to know.'

Grace stared at him in mounting horror as something occurred to her. Would it be impossible?

No, it wouldn't be impossible. It wouldn't be impossible at all.

Suddenly the pieces started to slot together like a jigsaw and the black, murky picture that began to emerge sickened her. Things that Rafael Cordeiro had said since she'd arrived came back to her, things that she hadn't understood at the time. *I don't know how you can sleep at night.*

It *could* have happened.

And now she knew *how* it could have happened.

She knew how, but not who.

Horrified and more than a little panicked, Grace was suddenly tempted to blurt out the truth but the grim set of his mouth prevented her from speaking. It was too late for the truth. You didn't have to be a genius with people to see that he'd already tried her and found her guilty. She could see the anger, raw and elemental, flickering deep in his eyes and suddenly she bitterly regretted not being honest at the beginning.

She should have told his business team all about her limitations from the start. She should have been open and honest. But if she'd told them, they never would have invested. Rafael Cordeiro would have written her off, the way everyone did.

Everyone, including her father.

And she was so used to covering up—so used to finding her own way round her problem—that she'd kept it a secret.

And she still couldn't quite believe what was facing her. Unwilling to accept what he was saying, she searched for alternative explanations and came up with nothing.

She swayed slightly and then felt strong male hands on her arms as Rafael forced her back into her seat.

'Sit down,' he said roughly, 'and try to get a grip. If you commit fraud you take your chances and deserve to be found out. These people are entirely innocent and your actions have brought them close to ruin.'

Grace licked dry lips, desperately trying to think straight. 'We buy our coffee from a company and we pay generously. Obviously they're not passing that on to the producer. They must be doing something with the money. They must be splitting it with someone in my company.'

Rafael gave a contemptuous smile. 'And I wonder who that could be? The owner, perhaps?'

She shook her head, too shocked and numb to muster a spirited defence. 'No. Not me.' *But who?*

What she really needed to do was go back through the company accounts in minute detail, but how could she do that?

Whom could she trust?

She almost laughed at the irony of the situation.

It was ironic that the one man who had the skills to help her was watching her with grim distaste. How much greater would his disapproval be when he knew the truth about her? To clear her name she had to tell him everything about herself and yet even as the thought entered her head, she dismissed it.

She'd never made excuses for herself and she didn't intend to start now. And anyway, the fact that she wasn't directly to blame didn't absolve her of responsibility.

Café Brazil was *her* business.

She'd been too trusting—and that misplaced trust had had disastrous consequences.

No, she couldn't ask Rafael Cordeiro for help any more than she could blame him for not agreeing to extend the loan. It was over. She'd go home, back to England, and somehow discover the answers she needed. And then she'd look somewhere else for the finance she needed to pull her company out of trouble.

CHAPTER FIVE

THE walk back through the rainforest to Forest Lodge was charged with tension, the atmosphere between them snapped taut after the outpouring of emotion at the *fazenda*.

And that was hardly surprising, Rafael said to himself as his long legs swallowed up the distance. Women were never at their best when they'd been found out. And Grace Thacker had been well and truly found out. There was no more hiding. Her fraud was exposed, the consequences of her actions thrust in her face. With him standing over her shoulder and Filomena crying, she'd had little choice but to express guilt and remorse and she'd done it most convincingly.

In fact, she'd been *extremely* convincing. If he hadn't known it to be impossible, he would have thought that the accusations levelled at her had come as a surprise. Indeed, her shocked response and her almost remarkable display of self-condemnation had both been sufficiently compelling to have him on the verge of reaching out with words of comfort and support.

He'd even run through the facts in his head one more time, just to be absolutely sure he couldn't have made a mistake. Was there any way she could be innocent of the fraud he'd uncovered?

The answer was no. There was no way. She had access to the accounts. She knew the company figures. In addition to that, the person in charge of finances at her company was her own father. So obviously it was a family job.

Glancing behind him, Rafael was surprised to see her right on his heels. He was walking fast but she, despite her lesser height and build, was keeping up.

And then he saw the emotion in her eyes and knew that she wasn't even aware of her surroundings.

Was it simply anger and frustration he was seeing? Probably. After all, her fraudulent money-making scheme had been exposed and terminated.

He had no doubt that her convincing display of regret at the *fazenda* had been played out for the benefit of Filomena and Carlos. Why was he impressed when he, better than anyone, knew just how well a woman could perform when she found herself in a tight spot?

Didn't he know better than anyone just how low a woman could stoop in order to yank herself from poverty to riches?

Grace Thacker's business was about to fold and, despite her impassioned request, he had no intention of throwing her the lifeline she so desperately wanted.

Rafael frowned and concentrated his attentions on the path ahead.

He'd arranged for the helicopter to collect her the following morning and fly her back to Rio de Janeiro so that she could catch a commercial flight to London.

Which meant that she had one more night in the rainforest to stew in her guilt.

Only he had no doubt that once she reached the privacy of her room she wouldn't be wasting time on emotional demonstrations of regret and remorse. Why bother if she didn't have an audience?

They arrived at the lodge and Rafael turned to her. 'You have two hours until dinner. I expect you'll want to rest.'

She didn't look as though she'd even heard him so he repeated the words and this time she glanced at him in shock as if she'd forgotten his existence. 'Sorry?' She blinked several times, clearly forcing herself to concentrate. 'Yes. Thank you.'

He still had a feeling she hadn't heard anything he'd said and he found himself noting the pallor of her skin and the dark shadows under her eyes. She looked stricken. Exhausted.

Rafael frowned. They'd walked miles in challenging conditions and she hadn't once complained but the physical challenge had to be taking its toll.

'You need to take a shower and lie down for a while.' Even as he spoke the words he wondered why he was bothering to show such solicitude and she must have wondered the same thing because her eyes widened.

'I'm sorry to inconvenience you by staying another night.' She was back to sounding like a polite child taking leave of a party and he found himself wishing she'd come back at him with the fighting spirit he'd grown accustomed to during their walk through the forest.

The woman was a mass of contradictions and almost impossible to read. She was a strange mix of humour and seriousness. Innocence mingled with an intense sexuality that seemed entirely unconscious. She didn't flirt and yet every movement of her body seemed to seduce.

Birds swooped over the lodge in a kaleidoscope of bright rainbow colours but this time their antics drew no gasp of delight from her. No acknowledgement and no questions. In fact she didn't seem to notice.

It was as if she was in shock.

'I'll meet you at dinner.' Up until that moment he'd had no intention of eating dinner with her and the flicker of surprise in her eyes told him that she was equally astonished by his invitation.

Why did he want to spend another evening with her? Why

not just walk away from her, relieved that the whole sordid matter had finally been cleared up? By the morning she'd be gone from his life.

Only he knew that shaking her off wasn't going to be that easy.

There'd been more to that kiss in the forest than just a steamy encounter between consenting adults. Far more.

Even now it was between them, shimmering like an invisible force, pulling them together. And she must have felt it too because she made a nervous gesture and backed away. 'Perhaps I should have dinner in my room. But I'd be grateful for the use of a phone. I'll reimburse you, of course.'

Given the sick state of her finances, he wanted to ask 'what with?' but he held the words back. 'There's a phone in your room. Use it, but you'll eat dinner with me.'

She didn't argue, apparently compliant, but he wondered whether she was just too worn out and ground down to argue. She seemed—defeated?

Which was a good thing, he reminded himself firmly, running a hand over the back of his neck to prevent himself from putting a hand on her arm. If her remorse and regret were genuine then she might even be put off doing a similar thing again.

Grace dropped the phone down into its stand and flopped back on the bed.

Nothing.

No one.

Her father was away on business and so was the manager she'd appointed to help with her business-expansion plan. She'd even tried ringing the dealer herself but had got no further than a message service.

The answers to the desperate questions that had formed in her mind were obviously not going to come easily. Especially not when she was thousands of miles away in the rainforest.

Right now she needed to be back in London, tracking down the person who was so cleverly defrauding her company.

But London was an eleven-hour flight from Rio and she was still in the jungle. And she still had a whole evening to get through. An evening with a man who had every reason to think that she was a nasty piece of work.

It was ironic, she thought helplessly, that the action which had finally confirmed to her that Rafael Cordeiro wasn't the cold-hearted man he was reputed to be was the very one that was going to deprive her of her beloved business.

He was going to withdraw his loan because he thought she'd hurt Carlos and Filomena. It hadn't been because he was determined to squeeze the last bit of profit out of her. It had been because he hadn't liked seeing her cheat those straightforward, honest people who were struggling to survive alongside nature.

And how could she blame him for that decision, given the facts at his disposal?

If he was right—and she had no reason to doubt him—then her company *had* cheated those people and the fact that she'd known nothing about it didn't excuse her. It was obvious that he cared about them deeply and the knowledge pleased her. *So he wasn't so damaged that he couldn't feel, was he?* There was good in him, if you bothered to look deep enough.

But that didn't help her business.

Everything she'd built was about to disintegrate into dust. People were going to lose their jobs and it was all her fault. She should have known. She should have noticed. *Except that she knew that there was no way she ever could have noticed.* She knew that.

Should she tell Rafael the truth?

But what was the point of that? Anything she said now was just going to look like an excuse. It was too late for explanations. Far, far too late.

She wanted to cry but the tears wouldn't come. Instead she lay there, numb, staring at the ceiling and trying to work out her next step, but lying still was impossible when she had so much pent-up emotion inside her.

She felt angry, confused, lost, afraid—but most of all she wanted answers. *She wanted to know who had done this to her.*

Unable to lie there when her life was falling apart, she sprang off the bed and paced across the bedroom, listening to the calls of birds and monkeys high up in the trees.

Suddenly she wanted to be out there too, back in the soothing, verdant rainforest where city life and corporate problems seemed so far away.

And then she remembered what Maria had said about the forest pool. Didn't they always say that exercise was good for relieving tension? Well, she'd swim and then maybe she'd be calm enough to sustain a conversation during an evening with Rafael Cordeiro.

If they didn't stray on to the subject of business, sex, love or marriage, they just might be able to keep the evening civil.

She slipped into her red bathing costume and pulled on the linen dress, reminding herself to be careful with it because it was all she had to wear for dinner.

Taking a towel from the bathroom, she pushed her feet into her shoes, carefully wrote something on her hands and made her way downstairs. Not trusting her directional skills, she wandered through the lodge to find Maria.

The housekeeper was in the kitchen, chopping a variety of exotic vegetables, but she willingly stopped when Grace asked to be reminded of the way to the pool.

She led her out through the glass atrium and onto a path that led away from the *fazenda* and into a different part of the rainforest.

Grace glanced to her left and right, delight mingling with

trepidation. It was the wildest and yet the most beautiful place she'd ever seen. Huge, exotic leaves rose upwards towards the light like spears while others nestled closer to the forest floor, so large that it was like taking a stroll through a giant's garden. Climbers scrambled up tree trunks and orchids and ferns clustered around the branches.

A flash of movement caught her eye and she paused, watching as a brightly coloured frog, tiny and delicate, clung to the tree trunk, and then there was a loud squawk from above her and a bird swooped up into the trees, its feathers a flash of red.

Parrot? Toucan? Assessing bird life as a suitably neutral topic for the dinner table, Grace made a mental note to steer the subject round to the wildlife over dinner. Then she concentrated on the route, noticing that they'd turned off the main path and were now walking along a narrow trail. Trees and ferns brushed against her arms and legs and in the background there was a rushing noise that grew louder as they walked.

Glancing over her shoulder, Grace tried to memorise the way back to the lodge.

And then the trees seemed to open up and the path widened. And there, in front of them, was the pool. Grace caught her breath in surprise and delight.

The frothy white waterfall poured over the rocks above and spilled into a large pool bordered by huge boulders and tall ferns. Surrounded by trees, exotic plants and birds and butterflies of every conceivable colour, the pool water gathered up the evening light and sparkled as though a million precious jewels lurked beneath the surface.

'It's beautiful.' She glanced around her and Maria nodded.

'It's safe, but not at night-time. And be careful walking back to the lodge. It's very easy to take the wrong path. Turn left and then right.'

Grace was looking at the pool. The walk through the jungle

and the shocking revelations about her business had left her feeling drained and exhausted. It would be a relief to strip off, cool down and relax. Then, perhaps, she'd be able to cope with the looming pressure of dinner.

And, after that, she'd work out what she was going to do, what exactly had gone wrong and how she was going to repay those people.

Rafael strode purposefully up the path that wound through the jungle to the forest pool.

Maria had interrupted his non-stop round of phone calls to inform him that Grace was swimming and he'd felt an immediate rush of irritation that she'd chosen that moment to wander off. His New York office was spearheading the negotiations for an extremely complicated deal and they were constantly clamouring for his input.

He could have left her on her own, of course. It was unusual for the local wildlife to explore that particular pool, but still…

He quickened his pace, noticing with an upward glance that it would soon be dark.

As if confirming his thought the lights by the side of the path suddenly gleamed and fireflies darted across his line of vision.

He came to the fork in the path and moments later he heard the rushing sound of the waterfall and pressed on through ferns, over huge, shiny boulders until he saw a flash of brilliant red. Like an exotic creature she slid through the pool, lithe and fit, her body slim and graceful, her blonde hair trailing loose in the water.

Hot molten lust erupted through his body and Rafael tucked his hands in his trousers and cursed softly, fighting against the impulse to join her because he knew that to join her would be to invite complications that he didn't need.

What he *did* need was uncomplicated sex, and he knew that he wasn't going to enjoy that with a woman like Grace Thacker.

She was the very worst sort of woman. It wasn't the greed that bothered him, he was used to that and he'd never found female greed to be a barrier to enjoyable sex.

He was even prepared to play their game, up to a point, which was why he was on good terms with most of the top jewellers in the world. No, it wasn't the greed that held him back. It was something else entirely. Grace was the sort of woman who not only expected you to hand out diamonds, but also wanted fake words of love and affection. She was the sort who dug and analysed and thought that there was an answer for everything if you only searched hard enough for it.

She wasn't the sort of woman to simply allow a relationship to be superficial.

Even now, floating in the pool, she appeared to be thinking. And then she opened her eyes and saw him. 'Am I late for dinner?' She swam across to him. 'Is it time to get out?' The late-evening sunshine bathed her body in a warm glow and the water clung to her hair like tiny beads of crystal.

Consumed by an attack of sexual hunger so intense that his body was ablaze with it, Rafael instantly redrafted his personal rules about women.

So she talked too much and was far too interested in what made him tick. *So what?*

He just needed to distract her and teach her that superficial could be good.

'It gets dark quickly in the jungle and the paths can be confusing. And the animals sometimes come and drink from the pool.' Until that moment he hadn't believed he could be so unsubtle. What was he hoping? That she'd leap screaming out of the pool and dive into his arms for protection?

Well, yes, actually. It would save her the bother of dressing just so that he could undress her again. And he *was* going to undress her. He'd made his decision. 'You never quite know what might be lurking in the pool. Piranha, anaconda, alligators…' He lingered over the words but she simply looked at him.

'Nothing more dangerous than that?' Her tone was weary and he was left with the distinct impression that she would have welcomed the arrival of something dangerous and deadly to distract her from her problems. Not only was she still in the pool, but she was positively luxuriating in the water as if she was indulging in some sort of private fantasy that she had no wish to abandon.

He frowned and worked a little harder. 'The occasional jaguar—'

'I like cats.'

He frowned. 'You're not going to get out?'

She gave a humourless laugh. 'What for? So that you can simmer and boil and intimidate me?'

'I *don't* simmer and boil and intimidate.'

'Yes, you do. But I don't blame you. I'd probably do the same in your position. It's nice to know that you care about something.'

Rafael gritted his teeth. *She was doing it again.* Worming her way into his mind when the only place he wanted her was flat on her back in his bed. 'You know nothing about me.'

'Well, that's true.' She floated on her back and her eyes drifted shut. 'You keep yourself shut away. Presumably you're afraid that someone might discover that you're actually a good person and that would damage your bad, dangerous image.'

'You talk too much,' he informed her in a driven tone and she opened her eyes.

'And you don't talk enough.' There was a faint smile on her lips. 'You know, if you just learned not to judge on appearances, you'd be almost human.' The dimple was back, he noticed, just above her mouth on the left-hand side. He stared at it, transfixed, and then decided that the conversation had gone far enough.

'Aren't you going to get out of the water?'

'I suppose so.' She pulled herself out of the pool, scooping her wet hair away from her face as she reached for her towel. 'Are you trying to frighten me with all this talk of animals, Rafael? Because you're wasting your time.'

He'd noticed. She'd tramped through the rainforest, fallen in rivers and walked past spiders the size of her hand, all without a word of complaint.

'You need to stay alert in the rainforest. There are plenty of hazards.'

'A bit like working in the commercial world, then,' she quipped, rubbing the towel over her limbs. 'Drop your guard for a moment and someone is waiting to eat you up in a mouthful and swallow your dreams whole.'

He found himself watching her every movement, the flow of her arms as smooth and graceful as a dancer's. The red swimming costume was moulded to every curve and the vivid colour seemed almost to be part of her, as if she were a jungle creature every bit as exotic as those that surrounded her. He might have thought she was relaxed and carefree if he hadn't seen the shadows in her eyes and the tension in her narrow shoulders.

Not so relaxed.

'Did you make your calls?'

'Yes.' She kept her smile bright as she swung the towel over her shoulders, concealing her high, firm breasts from his view. 'It seems that no one is in when the conversation topic is fraud. At least being in the jungle should give me a crash course in dealing with predators. Obviously, I need it.'

There was self-mockery in her tone, which he didn't understand. So she'd been found out? What was the problem? Weary of the act and wishing she'd just admit guilt so that they could get down to the important things in life, Rafael gritted his teeth.

'Who were you hoping to talk to?'

'Just about anyone, really.' She slid her feet into her shoes. 'My father. The dealer who sold us the coffee. But everyone has conveniently vanished. I suppose you could say that the rats are leaving the sinking ship.' She stared into the jungle and he thought he caught the sparkle of tears in her eyes. But then she turned to look at him and her smile was bright. 'My fault for being so trusting.'

She just wouldn't let it drop.

He stared at her with exasperation, wondering whether she really thought he believed any of her elaborate excuses. Not for one moment did he think she'd even tried to phone anyone. Why would she, when she was already in possession of all the answers? 'They could just be out.'

She nodded, apparently not picking up on the irony in his voice. 'I expect that's it.' Her eyes were tired and her tone formal, designed to keep him at a distance. For some reason that he couldn't identify, that distance annoyed him.

Suddenly he didn't care whether she was innocent or guilty. He just wanted her in his bed. As far as he was concerned, the rest of it was irrelevant.

So she was greedy and self-seeking—*what woman wasn't?*

'Shall we just change the subject?' he suggested helpfully, giving her permission to drop the act. He felt nothing but relief when she nodded.

'Yes. We're not going to discuss this again.' Her voice was firm and her chin was held at an angle that he was beginning to recognise signalled determination. 'The problem is no longer yours. I think that's one fact that we have managed to confirm.'

Finally, they were getting somewhere. 'Forget your business,' he purred, deciding that some reinforcement wouldn't go amiss. 'Move on in life. Do something else.'

'Oh, no—I couldn't possibly do that. It wouldn't be right. There are too many people depending on me and if I just give up, they're affected too.' She tilted her head to one side and shook it slightly, allowing her hair to fall in a damp mass over her shoulder. Then she twisted it into a thick rope, squeezing out the water with her hands. 'So I'm not going to give up. I'm going to find out who is guilty and try and recover the money. After that I'm going to apply for another loan, pay back Carlos and Filomena and carry on with my business.'

Frustrated that she was *still* trying to shift the blame onto someone else and totally bored by all talk of cafés and coffee when what he really wanted to do was drag her against him and taste her mouth again, Rafael decided that there was only one way to move the conversation forward to his satisfaction. 'I'll extend the loan,' he said smoothly. 'That way you can carry on playing cafés as long as you like.'

She paused but then shook her head. 'No, but thank you. It's a very generous offer.'

Not generous, Rafael thought, gritting his teeth. Selfish. He wanted her mind off her wretched business and onto something more worthy. Him. His eyes lingered on her mouth and he struggled to concentrate. 'It's my money. Giving it away is my choice.'

'And refusing is mine.' Her voice was soft. 'I don't want your money. In the circumstances it wouldn't feel right.'

As far as he was concerned there was only one thing that would feel right at that particular moment and it involved both of them naked on silk sheets. The reason for her presence here, the fraud, the deception, all of it had ceased to matter to him.

'In that case, let's agree to just drop the whole subject,' he agreed, glancing upwards with a frown. 'It will be dark in about ten minutes. We need to get back. You'll need time to change for dinner.'

'Oh, no—' With a cry of anxiety she bent down and picked up the dress that she'd laid on the rock. 'It's muddy. I must have splashed it when I was swimming.'

Rafael stared at her with a distinct lack of comprehension. 'And?'

'And it's all I have to wear!' She gave the dress a little shake and sighed. 'My combat trousers are wet and muddy, this is wet and muddy—'

'So it's naked, then,' Rafael suggested in a slow drawl, watching as the colour bloomed in her cheeks.

'I'll have to wear my suit...'

Struggling against the temptation to point out that clothes were largely irrelevant because he didn't intend her to stay dressed for long, Rafael took her arm and urged her down the path. 'Maria will find you a dress. Now move, or you might find that you're someone else's dinner.'

Grace sat on the edge of her bed, trying to stop worrying long enough to dress for dinner.

Had she been wrong to turn down his offer of financial help?

It was all very well having high standards, but what if no one else would loan her the money she needed? Those standards of hers would cost people their jobs.

Trying to rouse herself from her state of anxiety, Grace stared at the dress that Maria had delivered moments earlier.

It shimmered and shone, changing colour with the light, one moment pale turquoise and the next silver. It was, quite simply, the most exotic, beautiful dress she'd ever seen.

Not even wanting to think about the person it had originally belonged to, she slid it over her head, grimacing slightly as it clung to her hips.

Whoever had chosen this dress had been skinnier than she was, she thought ruefully, sliding the fabric over her hips and wondering whether it was actually going to be too tight. Assuring herself that it was a style that was supposed to cling, she turned sideways to look at herself in the mirror.

It was a dress designed to turn an ordinary woman into a film star, a dress designed for sin and seduction, and just wearing it put a smile on her lips.

Just for tonight she'd forget, she told herself, slipping her feet into her high-heel shoes and picking up her bag.

This one night in the jungle she was going to be the sort of woman who wore this sort of dress. She was going to forget about all her problems because despite empty assurances from Rafael Cordeiro she knew that there was no way she could solve them tonight. Tomorrow, along with reality, would come soon enough.

Tomorrow she'd be back in London. She'd track down the people who were so carefully avoiding her and she'd find out exactly what had gone wrong with her business. And her life.

Which meant that she had one more night in paradise.

CHAPTER SIX

RAFAEL WAS ALREADY seated at the table when she arrived on the terrace. He had a drink in his hand and his blue shirt was open at the neck and revealed just enough bronzed male flesh to draw her eyes for longer than she would have liked. Even dressed casually he looked cool, sophisticated and way out of her league.

She scanned his handsome features and her heart bumped crazily against her chest. What was it about him that had such a powerful impact on her?

She didn't know and she didn't understand it. But she knew that whatever had scarred him in the past, however bad his experiences had been, she didn't want him to think her guilty of fraud.

She hadn't intended to bring the subject up again but how could she not? No matter how hard she tried to push the whole thing away until tomorrow, the guilt kept intruding. 'You must think I'm awful,' she said impulsively as she slid into her chair, 'taking money from those people. I know that I'm sort of guilty because it's *my* company but I want you to know that I didn't know anything about it. I need you to believe that.'

He was still, his eyes on her face. He reminded her of a jungle animal, watching. Waiting for exactly the right moment to pounce. 'I believe you.' His low, smooth male voice flowed over her tattered nerves like healing honey.

'You do?' It wasn't the answer she'd been expecting and she couldn't hide her surprise or relief. 'You really mean that? I still don't know exactly who is responsible but I'll find out and change things. And I'll keep a firmer control on the figures. I should have noticed, I know, but—' She badly wanted to tell him the truth but she didn't want to sound as though she was making excuses.

'But when you're involved in the day-to-day running of the business, it's very easy to lose grip on the numbers.' He finished her sentence, his dark eyes velvety warm and surprisingly sympathetic.

'Yes.' That wasn't exactly what had happened, but it was close enough. And he seemed to understand. Which was a massive relief to her because for one horrible moment in the *fazenda* she'd thought that she was never going to be able to convince him that she hadn't deliberately taken money from anyone.

She still didn't know what it was that had made him so cynical and sceptical about people's motives but she was thoroughly relieved that at least he seemed to have absolved her of blame.

He'd obviously had time to think about everything she'd told him.

He was watching her now with a lazy, slumberous gaze and she felt herself relax.

'I should have been more careful,' she admitted, 'but I'm relieved you no longer think I was guilty of fraud.'

'I think we should now put the entire episode behind us.' His voice was molten sexuality, the gentle curve of his perfectly shaped mouth drawing her gaze. And it was impossible to look at his lips and not remember the kiss. The hot, fevered burn of his mouth on hers, the erotic stroke of his tongue and the firm, deliberate touch of his hands on her body.

As her body flared to life, she blinked with embarrassment and tried to shake off the memory.

Why was she suddenly thinking of nothing but that kiss? She should be worrying about her business and thinking about the future and instead her head was filled with memories of uncontrolled passion in the hot, humid rainforest.

Her life was now a mess of tangled problems and her brain should have been filled with numbers and solutions to those problems. Instead it was full of the wonder of that kiss and the sounds of love echoed in her head; *gasps, soft moans of encouragement, his voice, thrillingly deep and unfamiliar, urging her on...*

She shook her head to clear the vision. There was no point in remembering the kiss. No point at all. And no point in indulging in silly, girlish fantasies, she told herself firmly. He wasn't the right man for her and a little hot passion in the steamy jungle didn't change that fact.

Her world and his world didn't coincide.

'I haven't even thanked you for the dress. It's beautiful and it even fits—just.' She kept her tone light and smiled her thanks as Maria placed a drink in front of her. 'The owner was obviously a size smaller than me.'

'It looks better on you.' He lifted his glass in her direction and delivered a slow, appreciative smile that was unmistakably masculine. '*Much* better.'

His careless dismissal of the owner of the dress was completely in character and yet questions throbbed in her head and she bit her lip to hold them back.

Whose was it?

Did you love her?

Did you hurt her?

Did you look at her the way you're looking at me now?

Conscious of his gaze, Grace slid a hand over the shimmering fabric. 'I can't imagine why anyone would leave it behind.' It was the sort of dress that made a girl feel beautiful.

'The owner was in rather a hurry to leave. I seem to recall that jungle life didn't suit her.' His voice was a soft accented drawl and revealed nothing about his feelings or emotions but she knew—sensed without a shadow of doubt—that it wasn't jungle life that hadn't suited the owner of the dress but life with Rafael Cordeiro.

So he *had* hurt her. Clearly the girl had walked away without even pausing to pick up her belongings.

And knowing that, why was she still sitting here, allowing the atmosphere to pull her in? Why was she allowing him to draw her into the intimacy of his gaze? Knowing what she knew, just how much was she prepared to risk?

Her self-esteem?

A lifetime of pain for a moment's pleasure?

Her heart?

She pushed the question away. 'You're a very complicated man, Rafael.' Her voice was husky and she gave him a shy smile as she lifted her glass to her lips and sipped the wine. 'Cold and hot at the same time. You claim to not like people and yet there's kindness in you, I know there is.'

'Don't turn me into something soft and cuddly, Grace.' There was a warning in his voice and she smiled at the image that his words created because they were so far removed from reality.

'No, never that.' His steady gaze unsettled her. 'But you treated Carlos and Filomena with kindness and respect. And you clearly care about them or you wouldn't have been so angry with me.'

His eyes mocked. 'I'm a saint. I'm sure you've heard that about me.'

'I don't listen to gossip. I prefer to make my own judgements.'

'A woman who doesn't gossip?' He raised his glass in a silent toast. 'Are you a betrayer of your sex, Grace?'

'No. But I know that appearances can be deceptive. People

make judgements based on their own experiences. Isn't that what you did with me? When I arrived you made that comment about lying and cheating being part of a woman's genes. But you weren't born thinking that. Who made you think that, Rafael?'

He studied her for a long moment, his eyes lingering on hers as he considered her question. 'Perhaps you have escaped the lying and cheating gene but you seem to have more than your fair share of the psychology one. Why do you want to know about me, Grace?'

'Because I want to help.'

He gave a sardonic smile. 'Do I look as though I need help?' He leaned back in his chair and glanced around his surroundings and she understood the message in his gaze. Yes, they were in the jungle but that didn't for one moment detract from the luxury of his home or the abundant evidence of his extreme wealth. The clues were everywhere.

'I wasn't talking about money. *Obviously* you don't need money.'

'Then what do I need, Grace?' His soft tone bordered on the dangerous and his eyes warned her to drop the subject.

'Love.' She stumbled over the word. 'You need love. I don't believe your reputation or the image you portray. I've seen kindness and when it's anything to do with Brazil, your own country, you're passionate.'

He leaned forward, his eyes on her mouth. 'I'm not arguing that I'm passionate. I'm even prepared to demonstrate *how* passionate. And I'm more than happy to allow women to love me in any way they choose.'

She looked at the arrogantly arched brows, the roughness darkening his aggressive jaw and knew that he wasn't ever going to be an easy man to love.

Physically, yes, that would be no problem. Even if she hadn't heard the rumours she would have known that he was a hot-blooded, physical man. But nothing more than that. Nothing deeper. The barriers were up and he wasn't allowing her even a peep into his soul.

No one was allowed too close.

Flustered by how much she wanted to get close, she chose to change the subject. 'Do you often bring people here?'

'That depends on who they are and their purpose for visiting. The activities on offer here—' he smiled slightly as his eyes dropped to her mouth '—are limited.'

Her whole body heated under his lazy scrutiny and she shifted in her chair and reached for her wine. 'Did you build it?' Keeping the conversation moving and neutral was hard because she had the distinct feeling that he didn't want to talk at all. And he was looking at her in that way and all she really wanted to do was lean across the table and beg him to kiss her, *touch her,* the way he had in the forest.

And that impulse shocked her because she'd never felt that way about anyone before. Especially not anyone as hugely unsuitable as Rafael Cordeiro.

If there was ever a man designed to break a woman's heart, it was he.

'The lodge?' He was still looking at her mouth. 'Yes. I wanted somewhere that was inaccessible and private.'

'Because people bother you. Do you have family?'

'I don't give interviews, Grace. Not to colleagues, journalists—or lovers.' He lingered over the word as if testing the sound of it and her heart gave a little jump.

'But you can't live your whole life having nothing to do with people.'

'I have plenty to do with people,' his eyes lifted to hers, 'if they happen to interest me.'

Which basically meant anyone who made him money or warmed his bed.

That was what he was saying, wasn't it? Was he trying to shock her? Or was he making a proposition?

The heat pulsed through her and a dull ache spread across her pelvis. 'It must be nice to be able to escape. But you don't stop working, even here away from the city, bright lights and offices.'

The smooth lift of his eyebrows drew attention to the fact that she'd just revealed that she'd been watching him work.

'I couldn't sleep that well last night,' she confessed hastily, 'and I was looking out of my window. I saw you. Working on the computer. Talking on the phone.' Sleepless. Driven. *What were you thinking of down there in the dark with only a flickering screen for company? What demons robbed you of sleep?*

'I had work to do.' But the cold brevity of his statement didn't convince her and she sensed his withdrawal. Not physically. Physically he hadn't moved. But emotionally, something had shifted. The simmering connection between them was damped down by something cold and remote and she knew for sure that he lived with darkness. Something dark and painful that haunted him and she knew that his wakeful night had nothing to do with work and everything to do with his own personal demons.

Who had twisted his view of life?

Was it his wife or was it more?

She felt a flash of sympathy that she could neither prevent nor understand and it didn't make sense because if there was ever a man less demanding of sympathy then it was this one. But the desire to help in some way, to soothe and heal, was almost overwhelming.

She put her hands in her lap to prevent herself from touching him. 'Night-time is always the worse time,' she murmured. 'If there's a problem then it's magnified. There's no distraction.'

'Are you offering to provide me with distraction?' The demons were gone and now there was only the devil lurking in his eyes. A dangerous, wicked devil that danced and seduced and for a moment she couldn't breathe.

'I don't know you.' She was telling herself as much as him and he watched her, as if reading her thoughts.

'You know all you need to know.'

And what he meant by that, of course, was that she knew everything he wanted her to know.

And she realised that, for her, it wasn't nearly enough. She wanted more. She wanted to know more, everything there was to know.

How had that happened in just two short days?

How had she come to care for this man? Because she did. *Oh, yes, she did.* 'You're a difficult man to understand, Rafael.' Difficult. Dangerous. Deadly?

'I don't need you to understand me, Grace.' He smiled at her and there was something about that smile that robbed her of her ability to think clearly. It wasn't the smile of acquaintances or even friends. It was the smile of a lover. Intimate. Secretive. A smile that said *'I know what you're thinking'*.

And she truly hoped that he didn't because her thoughts were shocking.

She was stripping him naked again, as she had the day before, only this time the fantasy was fuelled by reality. This time she had some knowledge. She'd felt those skilled, purposeful hands on her flesh. She'd felt his hard mouth demanding submission. And she'd stroked her hands over the hard, honed flesh and muscle, now concealed by his shirt.

She shifted in her seat and the faint narrowing of his eyes told her that he'd observed the movement. And understood it.

He leaned forward and took her hand in his, his fingers toying with hers. 'It's almost painful, isn't it, this thing between us?'

She inhaled deeply and gave up on the food. There was too

much fluttering in her stomach to even contemplate eating. 'I don't know what you mean.'

'No?' He turned her hand, stroking her palm with his thumb, and the gentle, insistent pressure simply increased the tension inside her.

She had to look at him and immediately regretted the indulgence because once her gaze locked with his there was no looking away. His eyes demanded that she give up all her secrets and she obviously did because he gave a slow smile of satisfaction that was entirely masculine.

Trapped by that look, she tried to snatch her hand away. 'Don't look at me like that.'

'Like what?' His voice sounded impossible sexy and he held her hand firmly in his.

'As if you—'

'As if I want to strip that glittering dress from your body and carry on where we left off in the rainforest?' He leaned forward. 'I do, *minha paixao,* and so do you.'

There was no hiding from his meaning and she didn't even attempt to try. 'It would be ridiculous.' She breathed the words to herself but they seemed abstract, irrelevant because what was between them was out there, pulsing like a living force. To deny its existence would have been as futile as resisting and she discovered for the first time in her life that there were some forces that couldn't be resisted. 'Yesterday you thought I was a liar and a cheat.'

'Yesterday I thought you were beautiful and sexy. And I still think that today.' His voice stroked her like a lover's touch and she suddenly found it hard to breathe.

'I'm really glad you believe that I knew nothing about it. But it still doesn't mean—' she licked her lips '—I've never—'

'Acted on impulse? Followed your instincts? Why not?'

'Because the world doesn't work that way.'

His smile was derisive. 'And you care what the world thinks?'

'Yes, I suppose I do.'

His soft laugh indicated that her answer hadn't surprised him. 'Even if you do it can hardly matter out here. Tonight you're deep in the rainforest and the rest of the world is in another place altogether.'

It was true. She tilted her head back and listened to the sounds of the night that serenaded their intimate dinner for two. She felt as though nothing existed outside this jungle paradise with its bright rainbow birds, the dense greenery and the lush, exotic plants. And there was something about the closeness to nature that deepened the intimacy that was closing in on them.

'I've never followed an instinct that I don't understand. I don't know you and you don't even talk about yourself.'

He didn't contradict her. 'And that matters?'

'I don't feel safe with you.'

The humour in his eyes mingled with something much, much more dangerous. 'And is that what you demand from life, Grace Thacker? Safety?'

The pulse throbbed in the base of her throat and her voice was hoarse. 'Not right now.' Right now she wasn't thinking about safety. All she was thinking about was him. And the way he made her feel.

'If you want to choose safe then you'd better leave. I want you to be sure.'

Sure about what?

But she didn't even need to ask the question because the air was thick with the answer. It throbbed between them like a living force, drawing them together.

'I'm sure.' Her lips formed the words by themselves but strangely enough she had no wish to retract them. She'd never been so sure of anything in her life. And perhaps it was just being here, in the rainforest, so far removed from reality. But deep down she knew that it was nothing to do with her surroundings and everything to do with the man watching her.

He stood up and tugged her to her feet in a purposeful movement, not roughly but in such a way as to leave her in no doubt as to his intention. 'If you want to stop me, Grace, it has to be now.'

He was giving her a choice, then. *Or was he?*

Perhaps he knew that for her there had never been any choice. From the moment she'd seen him, standing with arrogant assurance in the doorway of the lodge, she'd been lost.

Could he see that? Could he see the effect he had on her? 'I want you.' The words were out before she could bite them back but she wasn't even sure that she would have done because something was driving her that she didn't really understand. A basic human instinct that being in this raw jungle had exposed?

He led her back through the glass dome and up a different set of stairs that opened into a bedroom not unlike hers. Only this one had a view of the waterfall and the forest pool, illuminated by tiny lights. She could hear the rush of the water punctuated by the insistent sounds of the forest that were becoming so familiar.

'It's amazing. It must be beautiful in daylight.'

'You'll have to tell me in the morning.' He closed the door so that it was just the two of them and the rainforest. 'It can be the second thing you see after you wake up.'

'The second?'

He drew her towards him, his fingers gently smoothing her hair away from her cheeks. 'The first, *minha paixao,* is going to be me.'

The breath caught in her throat and she lifted her face to his, waiting for his kiss, but he simply gave a slow, lazy smile and trailed his hand downwards to her neck, his fingers lingering on the tiny pulse that beat in her throat. 'Not yet. Nothing as good as this should ever be rushed.'

His touch soothed and seduced by equal measure and gradually the insistent rush of the waterfall and the night-time call of the rainforest faded to nothing. There was only him and the hot, swirling atmosphere sucking them both in.

Grace felt her eyes drift shut as time and thought were suspended. Her heart was thundering and her insides were melting and he'd barely touched her.

'You're beautiful.' He murmured the words against her throat and his fingers slid the glittering strap of her dress over her arm, exposing the curve of her shoulder. He smoothed a hand over her creamy skin, taking his time, savouring every millimetre of her flesh with the tips of his fingers. Her body hummed in response and her lips parted in a silent plea but still he didn't touch her mouth with his.

Instead she felt the nip of his teeth and the flicker of his tongue against her shoulder and then lower, to the soft hint of flesh that he'd exposed for himself by lowering her dress. His hands, so firm and confident, slid up her body and settled just above her waist and she gave a soft gasp as he dragged both thumbs over the tips of her breasts. Her nipples strained, seeking his attention, and he gave a low laugh of satisfaction and slid his fingers inside the clinging fabric, just as he had in the forest. Only this time it was different.

This time nothing was stopping them.

The atmosphere pulsed with a heat that was almost unbearable and she gave a low moan as the burning in her body intensified to almost unbearable proportions.

'You feel *so* hot,' he groaned, desire thickening his words and his accent, 'so beautiful.'

She hadn't even felt his hands on the zip of her dress but they must have been there because a slither of silk descending from her body to the floor announced to her fevered brain that she was now wearing only her lace panties.

'Rafael…' Consumed by an excitement so intense that it was almost terrifying, she lifted a hand to his cheek and he turned his head to kiss her hand, his eyes holding hers.

And then his mouth finally claimed hers.

His kiss was hot and passionate and without moving his mouth from hers he lifted her in his arms and placed her in the centre of the bed. He came down on top of her, his movements swift and possessive as he slid over her hips and shifted her under him.

She felt his weight, the pressure of his body on hers and her excitement increased because she was suddenly so aware of his physical strength. He lifted his head and rolled away from her, placing his hand on her quivering abdomen in a gesture that was unquestionably possessive.

As if to ensure that there was no mistake, he gave a slow smile. 'Mine,' he murmured softly as he moved his hand downwards in a purposeful movement. 'All mine.'

And she couldn't have argued with him even if she wanted to because she felt the hot, skilful slide of his fingers over her warm flesh—felt them move downwards in a remorselessly sensual exploration until they finally came to rest on the almost transparent wisp of silk that still protected her. His hand lingered for a moment, teasing, prolonging the agony, and then, just when she thought he was never going to touch her where she wanted him to touch her, his fingers moved and he removed the wisp of silk protecting her feminine secrets. The last barrier.

She gave a shiver and a gasp as a burst of almost agonising anticipation engulfed her.

He looked at her and then his gaze moved slowly downwards as he studied every part of her, his attention lingering on the golden shadows revealed by his fingers.

'Rafael…' She gasped his name and he shifted his body and lowered his mouth to her breast, his tongue and teeth grazing that sensitive part of her. Sensation shot through her body and she slid her fingers through his hair, wanting and needing to touch him, too.

With a low growl he turned his attention to her other breast, his tongue tasting and teasing until her pelvis burned and her hips wouldn't stay still, so desperate was she for satisfaction.

'You're incredibly sexy and responsive,' he groaned, moving slightly so that he could kiss her again. His mouth was hot and demanding and she felt the rough strength of his body pressing her back against the bed. Dizzy from his kiss, engulfed by sensation, Grace slid her hand down his back, feeling smooth flesh and hard male muscle.

She couldn't wait.

She didn't want to wait.

But he shifted his weight again, just slightly, and slid a hand downwards to the core of her femininity. She felt the skilled and gentle exploration of his fingers, his touch so sure and knowing that excitement ripped through her. Oblivious to everything except his control over her responses, she lay in a state of dazed excitement as he drove her to a peak of such delicious arousal that she was just desperate for release. Her hips moved and shifted, her back arched in silent invitation and she moaned his name in a plea for gratification.

And he gave a low groan of acknowledgement and slid his fingers deep. 'You are incredible, *minha paixao*. And I want you more than I've ever wanted a woman.'

She wasn't even listening. It was as if nothing could penetrate her brain except sensation and she couldn't concentrate on anything except the movement of his hands on her body.

And then the gentle, almost lazy, seduction ended and he shifted again. She felt his weight pressing her down onto the bed, his movements increasingly urgent as he repositioned her and parted her legs with his hand. The rough hairs on his thighs brushed against her skin and then she briefly felt the sensation of his velvety smooth erection brushing against her before he lifted her hips and entered her with a purposeful thrust.

Shocked by the sudden splinter of pain that stabbed her, she parted her lips in a gasp but his mouth silenced her and he kissed her, capturing every cry and every breath as he drove deep into her body, sending waves of frantic excitement rippling through her as he introduced her to an intimacy that was as alien as it was intoxicating. The pain was already a distant memory and she was aware only of throbbing masculinity, delicious sensations and an electrifying pleasure, as the initial discomfort was replaced by a burning fire that bloomed white-hot. She felt something deliciously unfamiliar build inside her, driven by the pulsing heat of masculine thrusts. He moved in a seemingly perfect rhythm, his body urging hers to respond, and she did.

Even without the slide of his hand encouraging her response, she found herself wrapping her thighs around his body, offering herself. And he took what she offered with an almost violent hunger, his sexual demands so great that she felt the room spinning and her heart pounding. It was electrifying, rousing and totally all-consuming and she held on, unsure where he was taking her but trusting him not to let her fall. Sensation devoured her like a greedy animal and she felt her body throb and sing until she was blind with need.

And he took her higher still, winding her body tighter and tighter until she teetered on the edge of something deliciously dangerous and unfamiliar from which there was no going back.

And with a sudden increase in tempo he sent her over the edge into a thrilling and terrifying vortex that consumed her body and threatened to engulf her forever. Her body contracted around his and she saw flashes of light, heard him mutter something in harsh tones and then felt the hot liquid burst of his own release. And then there was nothing but sensation, so agonisingly prolonged that if he hadn't been holding her she would have been terrified.

She clung to his shoulders and eventually the world around her calmed. She felt the pounding of his heart and the slick warmth of his skin against hers as they both struggled to recover sufficiently to move.

But he didn't move far. Instead he just rolled onto his back, pulling her with him so that she was still wrapped around him.

Still dazed and shocked by the intensity of the experience, Grace lay unsure what to say. And it soon became clear that speech wasn't necessary because he clearly had no desire to indulge in conversation.

Instead he closed his hands over her hips and moved her so that she straddled him. Her hair flowed onto his chest and he gave a slow smile and lifted his hands to her face.

'That was amazing, *minha paixao.*'

They were surrounded by the heat, sounds and rhythms of the jungle but all she could focus on was the hardness of his body, the touch of his hands and her own, burning excitement driving her on.

She couldn't get enough of him.

The connection between them was so intense, so perfect, that it was as if nothing outside the rainforest existed for either of them.

CHAPTER SEVEN

GRACE awoke to the sounds of the rainforest all around her and opened her eyes with a smile on her lips.

Was there any better place to wake up?

She was on her side and Rafael was lying next to her in a careless sprawl, one of his legs trapping her to the bed, as if to prevent her escape. But she had no plans for escape. At that moment she knew that there was nowhere else she'd rather be. No other man she'd rather be with.

Perhaps it was because they were both a little damaged, she thought, unable to resist stroking a hand over his shoulder. His skin was bronzed, a legacy of the sun and his Brazilian heritage, the muscle clearly defined and unmistakably masculine.

He had an incredible body and it was obvious to anyone fortunate enough to look at him that he was a very physical man. A man with strength who pushed and tested himself.

'You're staring at me.'

She hadn't even realised that he was awake. She moved her gaze from his shoulders to his face and saw that he was looking at her. His eyelashes, so thick and dark, all but concealed his expression and suddenly she felt impossibly shy.

'It must be late. We ought to get up. Your pilot will be here soon and I still have to gather up all my things.'

'My pilot is in Rio. Your things are all here. Maria brought them over last night.' He gave a lazy, satisfied smile. 'This is your bedroom now.'

What was he talking about? The night was over.

And somehow in broad daylight she felt so much more self-conscious than she had last night in the mysterious dark.

As if sensing her confusion, he pushed her onto her back and slid his hand over her abdomen and on to the curve of her hip in a gesture that was unmistakably possessive. 'I cancelled the helicopter. There's nothing to get up for.'

She felt a flicker of disquiet. 'You *cancelled* it?'

'Of course.' He delivered that confirmation in a tone of arrogant assurance. 'Did you really think that I was going to let you just fly home?'

Her heart banged crazily against her chest. 'It didn't occur to me that you'd want me to stay.'

'How could you doubt it?' With his customary decisiveness, he rose over her and lowered his mouth to hers, coaxing her lips apart with his. His kiss was demanding, hotly sexual and an explicit reminder of everything they'd shared the night before. And she kissed him back, her head spinning and her body bursting into flame in an instinctive and uncontrollable response to his touch.

The chemistry between them flared into something violent and powerful and he muttered something in Portuguese and parted her thighs with a firm and deliberate movement of his hands.

'Fly home? I don't think so. I want you,' he breathed against her mouth, 'isn't it obvious? Can you feel what you do to me?'

She felt what she did to him—felt him, hard and ready, and she gave a soft moan of excitement as she felt the blunt tip of his erection touching her intimately. She lifted her hips and felt him slide full-length inside her, his body taking instant posses-sion of hers in a smooth, confident movement.

'Rafael…' She moaned his name as he drove into her with bold, sure strokes that sent frantic waves of excitement pounding through her quivering body. She couldn't think or breathe and she wrapped her legs around him and clutched the slick, hard muscle of his shoulders, trying to hold on. *Trying to stop herself from falling.*

He gave a low laugh and nipped at her neck with his teeth. 'You would leave me, *minha paixao?* You want me to invite the helicopter to come?' His voice was rough with his own arousal and he slid an arm beneath her hips and altered the rhythm.

Hard and fast became slow and sensual and her body trembled and throbbed under the demanding pressure of his.

'No.' *She couldn't think about that now.* She couldn't think about anything except the hard, insistent demands of his body inside hers. 'No helicopter.'

He controlled her utterly, until she could no longer speak, until she wasn't even sure who she was any more.

And then he changed the rhythm again, dragging her upwards to a place so shockingly high that the fall back to earth could only be terrifying. Stars flashed in her head, bright and distant, and she dug her nails into smooth male flesh, holding on. Afraid to let go.

But he drove her to the very edge of that precipitous drop with a series of demanding, masculine thrusts that rode over her feeble resistance until she was aware of nothing but sensation. It was fast, desperate and primal and for a moment she hovered on the edge of ecstasy, clinging to the last threads of sanity. And then he urged her past the point of safety and there was an explosion of bright lights as her body splintered into a million glorious pieces. She held him, feeling the violent shudders of his body that signalled his own release. And for endless moments they clung together, locked in a volatile intimacy that devoured both of them.

Finally the storm receded and she was aware of his weight, of the slick warmth of his flesh against hers. *Of his masculine strength.*

The frantic pounding of her heart slowed and she opened her eyes to find him looking down at her with those brooding dark eyes that always made her think of danger.

'You're mine,' he said thickly, shifting slightly so that his mouth hovered just a breath away from hers. 'Remember that.'

He dropped his forehead onto her shoulder and then rolled onto his back, taking her with him. His breathing was unsteady. 'Not only are you not leaving the rainforest,' he murmured, stroking her damp hair away from her face with a gentle hand, 'but you're not leaving my bed. I'm keeping you here. Naked.'

Dizzy with happiness, her body still humming from the skill of his seduction, she gave a weak smile. 'You're talking like a caveman.' But she didn't even care. *It felt so good to be held.* 'I don't have any clothes anyway. A suit that you hate, a dress that's ruined and a pair of combat trousers that look as though they've been worn through the middle of the jungle. I can't think why.'

'You were amazing yesterday, have I told you that?' He shifted his weight slightly. 'I don't know any other woman who would have done what you did without complaining. Even when you fell in the river you refused my help. In fact you glared at me.'

'I didn't dare complain when you were already so angry with me.' The memory put a slight scratch in the perfection of the day and he frowned slightly, as if he, too, was resenting the reminder of their differences.

'That's behind us now.'

'Well, not exactly. We can't just forget it.' Reality intruded along with the sun's reminder that it was a new day. 'Whether we like it or not, it's morning. I have things to sort out. Important things. I feel very responsible.'

'I will make some calls,' Rafael assured her with his usual

confidence. 'The dealer who sold you the coffee won't be in business after today. I'm sure you would never have agreed to this deception had he not pushed you.'

Grace lay still for a moment, digesting his words. 'But I didn't agree to it. You say that he's overcharging and keeping the profit and I have no reason not to believe you, but if he's splitting that profit with someone then it certainly isn't me.'

Rafael hesitated and something close to anger flickered in his eyes. Then he gave a faint shrug and slid his hand down her body in a possessive gesture. 'Let's not have this conversation again, *minha paixao*. It isn't relevant any more. It's in the past. Over. As you said to me, everyone makes mistakes.' He gave her what she presumed was supposed to be an understanding smile. 'I'm sure you've learned your lesson. Don't cheat unless you're prepared to be caught.'

Grace felt as though she'd been showered with cold water.

He still thought she was guilty. *He'd slept with her thinking she was a liar and a cheat.*

'I don't believe this.' She sat up in bed and pushed his hand away, her breathing suddenly rapid and her heart pounding against her chest as the implication of his words sank in. 'You still think I'm guilty, don't you?'

His gaze was wary. 'Grace—'

'You still think I stole money from the company.'

His driven sigh made it clear that this topic of conversation was not of his choosing. 'You *admitted* your guilt.'

Had she? Had she ever said that? She rewound the conversations that they'd had on the topic. 'I said I felt responsible and I do, but not because I took the money myself. Because it's *my* company, so I'm ultimately responsible for everything that happens within it.'

He waved a hand in a dismissive gesture designed to silence her. 'It really doesn't matter.'

'It *does* matter because I have to go home and sort it out.' She tried to swing her legs out of the bed but he caught her in his arms and flattened her to the bed with his body. His weight and his powerful frame made sure that she had no option but to lie there.

'You're not leaving. I don't care what you did or didn't do. Can't you understand that?' His tone was harsh and impatient. 'None of this makes any difference whatsoever to the way I feel about you. It has absolutely no impact on what we share.'

'How can you say that?' She stared up at him, appalled and just hating herself for the immediate flare of heat that erupted in her pelvis. 'Are you seriously suggesting that you could just as soon sleep with a liar and a cheat as you could a decent, honest woman? Don't you have any morals?'

One bronzed shoulder lifted in a careless dismissal of her question. 'It is sex, *minha paixao.* Sex. I am only interested in what you do in my bed. What you do in your own time is really no concern of mine.' He frowned slightly. 'Providing, that is, you don't defraud Carlos and Filomena. But we both know that won't happen again.'

Appalled and horrified, she closed her eyes briefly, her fleeting happiness brutally punctured by his cynical attitude. 'I thought you trusted me.'

'Why would I *need* to trust you?' He seemed genuinely astonished by the question, the incredulity in his dark eyes betraying the fact that trust was an entirely alien concept to him. 'I was sharing hot sex with you, not giving you my investments to manage.'

She gave a soft gasp of pain and shook her head in disbelief. What insane magic had overtaken her in this enchanted forest? At what point had she lost her mind? What arrogance had led her to believe that she understood this man?

'Who did this to you?' Blinking back tears, she stared up at him, searching for some sign of softening or gentleness. But his face was all hard, strong lines. 'Who made you feel this way about people? About women?'

The sudden tension in his powerful shoulders betrayed his less than enthusiastic response to her question. 'Why do women always want to discuss the competition? You're the one lying naked next to me at the moment. That should be enough for you.'

For some unfathomable reason she felt a lump lodge in her throat. 'I feel sorry for you. You expect so little.'

'I'm extremely realistic about women. I don't expect more and I don't want more.'

'Well, I do.' She pushed at him, her fingers tangling with the rough dark hair on his chest. 'I do, Rafael. I need a great deal more than that.'

He didn't budge. 'What woman doesn't? And you will have it,' he promised, his voice low and seductive. '*Everything* you want. I think you'll find me an incredibly generous lover.'

His words were like a caress but this time she tried to ignore the immediate response of her body. 'Generous? Do you really think I'm talking about money?'

'Not just money,' he purred, his lingering kiss on her shoulder leaving her in no doubt as to what form his other expression of generosity was going to take.

Thoroughly agitated now, she wriggled away from him. 'I don't want your money! I want you to trust me. I want you to believe that I'm innocent. There must be some way of proving that I wasn't involved—that the money wasn't paid out to me. I want you to look at the figures again.'

Bored and visibly irritated, he gritted his teeth. 'The only figure I'm interested in is yours, *minha paixao,* naked and underneath me.' As if to emphasise his point, he slid a leisurely hand down her body from waist to thigh. 'None of the rest of it matters.'

'It matters to me.'

'Forget your business,' he ordered, leaning forward to drop a kiss on her mouth. 'You don't need it any more.'

'Of course I need it.' The business was her life. Her future. He had no idea what it meant to her. 'How can you even say that? Why would I just give it up?'

Rafael gave a slow smile, his mouth tantalisingly close to hers. 'Because you now have an alternative, and far more lucrative, source of wealth.'

She stared at him, her mouth falling open as she digested his words. 'You think I'd take your money? Do you think I even *care* about your money? *Do you think that's the sort of person I am?*' Did he know so little about her? And then she closed her eyes, realising just how little he did know about her.

And was that really his fault?

Wasn't that one of the risks you took when you allowed blind, furious passion to overwhelm rational thought? The truth was that common sense had been devoured by the pounding heat of the rainforest and an irresistible chemistry.

And yet for her it was more than chemistry. So much more.

She knew now that somehow, however improbable, she loved him—this hard, damaged, unsuitable man living in this remote jungle paradise. Unbelievable. And yet it had happened. She'd managed to fall in love with him.

Not with the cold, ruthless face he presented to the world. That face, no matter how handsome, didn't appeal to her. No, she was interested in something much deeper. She was interested in the man she saw beneath the barriers he'd erected. She'd only been afforded glimpses but it had been enough.

And if he never revealed more of himself then that was fine. She accepted him as he was. Loved him as he was.

Perhaps because she herself hid so much inside, she'd sensed a pain deep within him.

She'd felt a connection.

And somehow, she'd tumbled deeply in love with a man who didn't want her love.

He didn't want anyone's love.

Even when he'd been cold and ruthless, however, part of her had reached out to him.

His careless shrug betrayed his lack of insight into her feelings. 'I may be a cynic about love but that doesn't mean I don't understand what women need. You're amazing in bed. Last night really blew me away. For the foreseeable future I don't want you focusing your attention on anything but me.'

Knowing what needed to be done, she shook her head. 'That isn't going to be possible.' Last night was over and the magic of the rainforest was coming to an end. 'I need to sort out this problem. I have to sort it out. I promised Filomena and Carlos.'

How could she have been so stupid?

How could she have been so naïve, so egotistical, as to think that she could change this man whose entire reputation was based on his inability to feel a single thing for anyone?

She'd thought that there was hope for him—that there was a chink of kindness.

She'd even been arrogant enough to believe that she'd made a connection with him that no other woman had ever made.

Which made her nothing short of stupid and because of that she probably deserved all the pain she was feeling now.

There was a frown in his eyes, as if he didn't understand her. *And he didn't,* she thought, biting back hysterical laughter. Despite what she'd thought last night, he didn't even come close.

His eyes glittered dark with growing irritation. 'I'm merely making the point that you won't find yourself short of money.'

'So you're going to pay me for sleeping with you, is that what you're saying?'

Sensing danger, he narrowed his eyes and finally rolled away from her. 'No, that isn't what I'm saying.'

'Isn't it?' Dizzy from the speed with which the atmosphere had changed from loving to recriminatory, she sat up, trying to ignore the rising sickness in her stomach. 'But aren't you offering me an income? Gifts? More money than I can possibly spend in normal opening hours?' Her sarcasm seemed lost on him. He lay sprawled on the bed, watching her through heavy-lidded eyes, a faintly derisive smile touching his mouth.

Gone was the warmth and the lazy atmosphere of seduction. He was cold with her. Remote. Even a little—*bored?*

'Of course. Feel free to allow your most avaricious fantasies to envelop you.'

Anger shot through her, the emotion intensified by her own frustration with herself. 'My fantasies at the moment involve dropping you naked into a pool of extremely hungry piranha!' Flinging words like stones, she jumped out of bed and reached for her combat trousers. She dragged them on, ignoring the muddy stains in her haste to dress. Suddenly being naked and in the same room as him seemed completely inappropriate. 'I really thought that there was hope for you! I thought that underneath that hard outer shell you present to the world there lay a decent human being. Damaged, maybe. But buried there somewhere. And now I discover that you're just as cold and empty as you appear.'

His eyes narrowed. 'You are behaving like a child in a tantrum and it's unnecessary. I say again, I really don't care that you took the money. It's in the past and I never dwell on the past.'

'Yes, you do! It's dwelling on the past that makes you so cynical and suspicious.' She reached for her shirt, which lay discarded over the back of a chair. '*I did not take the money.*' She spread her hands in a gesture of helplessness and frustration. 'Why am I even bothering saying that to you when it's so obvious that you just can't see good in anyone? Well, I'm sorry for you, Rafael. *Really* sorry for you. I don't know what she did to you but she obviously did it well.'

The sudden flash of anger in his eyes made her freeze to the spot and for a moment they just stared at each other, the tension simmering between them like a living, breathing force. And then she saw the now familiar glitter in his eyes and felt the colour touch her cheeks.

Heat mingled with pain and it was a physical effort not to step towards him.

'How can you do that?' Her voice was soft, but her hand shook as she quickly jammed her arms into the sleeves, concealing her body from his appreciative gaze. 'How can you look at me like that when you think I'm guilty of stealing? Don't you have any standards? If you truly believed that of me you should have thrown me out, not taken me to your bed.'

His gaze was hard. 'Since I have no wish to live the life of a monk, my standards are realistic. As I said when you arrived, you're a woman. All women practise deception of one form or another. It really doesn't bother me,' he assured her in a confident drawl. 'I expect it.'

'You *expect* women to deceive you?'

'Women are greedy.' He shrugged. 'And manipulative. And very upset when things don't go their way, as you obviously are now.'

'You know what?' Her voice was so clogged with tears that she could hardly form the words. 'You're right that I'm upset. I'm *very* upset. Because last night was special for me. Really special. And now I discover that I was nothing more than a convenient female body in a slinky dress.'

He lounged back against the pillow, watching her as though she were a floorshow laid on for his entertainment. 'You're stunning when you're angry, *minha paixao.*'

'Then prepare yourself to be knocked flat by my beauty—' she jammed her feet into her shoes '—because I haven't even *started*. And what does that mean, anyway? You keep calling me that—'

'*Minha paixao?*' He shrugged, looking every inch the arrogant Brazilian billionaire. 'My passion.'

Great, she thought. *Passion.* Not 'love' or 'darling' or even 'sweetheart'. Not even in the throes of abandoned sex did Rafael Cordeiro make a mistake about the nature of the relationship.

Evidently bored with the direction of the conversation, he ran a hand over his face and stifled a yawn. 'I probably should have warned you,' he said softly, 'but I hate emotional scenes.'

She yanked her suit from the hanger and stuffed it into her bag. 'I just bet you do. In fact you hate everything that has a breath of emotion connected to it because emotions make you uncomfortable, don't they, Rafael?' She grabbed the linen dress and stuffed it into the bag after the suit, uncaring about the future state of either of them. 'You can walk through a jungle full of predators and it won't raise a sweat or a kick in your pulse rate, but stick an emotion in your path and all of a sudden you're on full alert in case it jumps up and bites you.' She yanked the zip of the bag so violently that it was a wonder it didn't object by breaking. Then she snapped the bag shut and slung it over her shoulder, glaring at him. She was so upset that she felt as though her whole body was on the verge of explosion. She didn't know whether to sob or scream but she wasn't going to do either with him watching. 'You're a snake, Rafael. Worse than anything the rainforest has to offer. And do you know something else? You may be an incredible lover but you're emotionally sterile. You're not capable of feeling *anything,* are you? Well, you'd better call that helicopter back, because our *passion* is well and truly over.'

She left the room without glancing back at him, wondering where to go while she waited for the helicopter to arrive. And it would arrive, she knew that. Now that their fragile relationship had been torn to shreds, it wouldn't be long before she heard the sound of an engine overhead.

He'd want her out of here, away from his private hideaway, so that he could get back to licking his wounds in private.

But she couldn't even focus on his wounds at the moment because her own were so deep.

One thing she knew, she didn't want to be anywhere near him while she waited.

Rafael lay on top of the rumpled bed, his eyes fixed on the trees that provided the view from his bedroom as he tried to identify the unfamiliar feelings inside him.

Completely unaccustomed to reflection or self-analysis, he gave up almost instantly.

She was right, he told himself. He *was* emotionally sterile. Completely unable to feel anything. But why did she think that was a bad thing? As far as he was concerned, it was fine. That was the way he wanted it. In fact, he'd worked really hard to achieve that state of equilibrium.

And last night had been amazing.

The sex had been incredible. Mind-blowing. And surprising. One moment she was shy, the next gloriously uninhibited.

He gave a brief frown. There'd been a moment when he'd actually wondered whether she was a virgin but her response had been so hot and passionate that he'd dismissed the thought almost instantly. No virgin would have responded to him the way she had and he'd simply made a mental note to take things a little slower the next time.

The sexual explosion that had consumed them had been every bit as powerful as he'd anticipated and he'd found himself looking forward to a feast of endless hot sex that would continue until he grew bored with her.

Looking at the door, which she'd closed firmly behind her—so firmly that the entire building had rattled—he wondered with weary resignation what had possessed him to think that life could be that simple.

When, with a woman, was life ever simple?

And despite the fact that Grace Thacker was surprising in many ways, deep down she was the same as the others.

Not just because her goal in life was clearly financial gain without any degree of effort, but because she played the usual games that women always did when going to bed with a man. Why weren't they ever just straightforward? Why couldn't chemistry just be chemistry and not have to be twisted into a Happy-Ever-After?

Driven by frustration, he sprang out of bed and prowled around the bedroom, trying to sort out his thoughts.

She'd accused him of emotional sterility but couldn't he also accuse her of emotional dishonesty?

What they shared was sex and nothing more.

So why couldn't she admit that instead of making everything so complicated?

What possible relevance did his emotions have in the context of their relationship? Her only interest in him should be in his physical stamina and the size of his wallet and, as far as he was concerned, he excelled at both. So why did she persist in her tiresome crusade to persuade him of her innocence?

Surely taking her to bed had more than proved that he didn't care about her intrinsic greed? That he was more than willing to accept her as she was.

What was her obsession with innocence?

Unless she was, quite genuinely, sorry for what she'd done. Either way, as far as he was concerned, it was finished.

Today he was going to make it his personal mission to ensure that the dealer's career in greed and deception was abruptly ended.

Like a man on a mission, he strode off to his office to make some phone calls.

CHAPTER EIGHT

DESPERATELY upset by their confrontation, Grace walked quickly into the forest, following the path to the waterfall and pool that had proved so tranquil the evening before.

What right did she have to be upset?

What right?

Had he made her promises? No, he hadn't.

So why did she feel so let down, so completely disappointed?

Because she'd thought she'd seen something in him.

She'd never felt so confused in her life. Her newly awakened body was humming and part of her wanted to rush back to the lodge, crawl into bed beside Rafael and forget the complications of her life. He was able to see their relationship in simple, straightforward terms—so why couldn't she?

The answer to that lay in the fact that there was one fundamental difference between them.

Despite everything that had happened in her life, she'd never lost hope, whereas Rafael…

She felt something sad inside her as she finally acknowledged the truth about him. Rafael appeared entirely disillusioned with women and life in general. Somewhere in his past, he'd lost all hope.

She walked on, her vision blurred, and it took about twenty

minutes for her to realise that there was no sign of the forest pool. Nor could she hear the waterfall. Which meant that somehow, somewhere, she'd taken the wrong path.

Ignoring the flicker of unease that sprang to life inside her, she stopped and looked around her, searching for something, anything, that she recognised, but it was all horribly unfamiliar.

Had they come this way the day before?

Had she passed the forest pool without even realising?

Deciding that her best option was to turn round and retrace her steps, she plodded back along the path, suddenly aware of all the shrieks, calls and sounds that filled the air around her. The leaves and branches beside her feet seemed to rustle and above her she saw a large spider, clinging to its web.

Yesterday, with Rafael's powerful body striding ahead of her, she'd felt strangely secure. Now, totally alone in the dense, almost oppressive rainforest, she felt a flicker of fear that she struggled hard to contain.

Panicking would get her nowhere, she reminded herself firmly, but then stopped in despair as the path forked. Left or right? She didn't remember even seeing a fork in the path on the way. And now it was almost impossible not to panic.

She couldn't be that far from the lodge, she reasoned, giving the spider a wide berth. She'd been walking for less than half an hour. Which meant that sooner or later someone would come and find her.

Or would they?

Was Rafael tucked up in front of his computer screen, working, oblivious to the fact that she was even missing?

It didn't make sense.

With mounting frustration, Rafael dropped the phone back onto his desk and stared out of the window, his mouth set in a grim line.

Now what?

He'd spent an hour on the phone and it had proved to be the most exasperating and perplexing hour of his life. And, far from being answered, the questions had multiplied. The manipulation of the figures went deeper than he'd first imagined.

But one thing had come through loud and clear. At no time had Grace Thacker been a beneficiary of the money that had been removed from the company.

Which meant that she'd been telling him the truth all along.

He ran a hand over his face and cursed softly as he forced himself to face facts.

She hadn't stolen anything, nor was she guilty of fraud and deception.

Which made her not dishonest, but quite astonishingly naïve.

He found it impossible to comprehend that she hadn't noticed the discrepancies in the company accounts. She was young, yes, but she was running a business. How could she not have suspected? Hadn't she looked?

Trying to curb his mounting frustration, he leaned forward, jabbed a button on his phone with an impatient finger and simmered at his desk until Maria appeared.

'Ask Miss Thacker to join me.' He spoke in Portuguese, his voice silky smooth, and his fingers drummed a steady rhythm on the table. She had the answers he needed, he was sure of it. It was simply a case of asking the right questions and, up until now, he clearly hadn't been doing that.

'Miss Thacker has gone into the forest.'

Little Red Riding Hood, escaping from the wolf.

Rafael's hand stilled and a frown touched his brows. 'She's gone for a swim again?'

Maria shook her head. 'I don't think she had a costume with her.' The housekeeper hesitated. 'And she looked a little upset.'

Not pausing to question why the opinion of his housekeeper

should suddenly matter to him, Rafael shot to his feet, cursing softly. 'How long ago?'

'Maybe half an hour?'

Long enough for her to have got into serious trouble. What had possessed her? Why had she just wandered off like that?

But he knew the answer to that, of course. She'd repeatedly pleaded her innocence and he hadn't believed her. She'd wandered off because she was upset and *he* was the one who'd upset her.

By not trusting her.

But *why* would he have trusted her, he asked himself savagely, when he'd never had reason to trust a single woman in the past?

Without wasting time indulging in the type of analysis and reflection that he considered to be a complete waste of time, Rafael strode out of the lodge and followed the ancient path that led deep into the rainforest. In parts it was barely passable and the tension in his shoulders increased as he contemplated what might have happened to a woman with no experience of the jungle. *A woman who was upset and not concentrating.*

He called her name but there was no response and he felt something uncomfortable shift inside him as he thought of the dangers of the rainforest.

Venomous spiders, snakes—

And then he gave a silent, self-deprecating laugh as the truth stared him in the face. She'd chosen to face all those rather than risk bumping into him again. So what did that say about him?

That he was a man any decent, honest woman would do well to avoid, and he knew, now, that Grace Thacker was a decent, honest woman. Naïve? Hopeless with figures? Too young and inexperienced to be running a business? Stupid?

Maybe one, if not all, of those things, but dishonest—no.

And this time, when she talked, he was going to listen. Properly. He was going to treat her carefully because clearly she was completely ill-equipped for surviving in the corporate jungle.

Guilt, uncomfortable and unfamiliar, scraped over his nerve-endings and he quickened his pace in the hope that exercise might relieve his growing tension.

He'd warned her, hadn't he? He'd revealed the man he was right from the start. There was no way she could accuse him of deception or even insincerity.

She'd come to him of her own free will and he wasn't to blame if she'd imagined something deep inside him that he knew just wasn't there. Was he responsible for the fact that she'd credited him with a depth of feeling when he knew that there was only emptiness inside him?

Whose fault was that?

His for allowing cynicism to blind him, or hers for allowing naivety to let her imagine qualities that he didn't possess?

He was so lost in the darkness of his own thoughts that he almost didn't notice her, sitting on a fallen tree trunk, her face pale.

He gave a low growl. 'What the *hell* were you thinking of, walking into the rainforest?' Anger erupted inside him with explosive force, all his promises to treat her carefully vanishing in his relief at finding her apparently unharmed.

'Rafael…' Visibly startled, she began to stand up but then his gaze flickered to something moving above her and he froze, his hand sliding to the stick that he carried in his belt.

'Stay still!'

He saw her narrow shoulders tense but she did as he ordered and he stepped forward and used the stick to carefully move the black and yellow snake away from her shoulder.

She turned her head slowly, her eyes widening as she focused on the thick, exotically coloured snake that slowly climbed the tree next to her. 'Is it poisonous?'

'No. But I didn't think you'd appreciate a three-metre-long snake snuggling into your lap.' The glassy pallor of her skin fuelled his temper. 'It *could* have been poisonous, Grace.'

More unsettled by that thought than he would have believed possible, he reached down and yanked her to her feet, his eyes blazing into hers.

'What did you think you were doing? This is the rainforest, not Bond Street. You don't just go for a gentle stroll!'

'I know that.'

'Then what the hell were you doing walking along this path?' He'd just removed a snake from within inches of her neck. Why wasn't she clinging to him or screaming hysterically? It occurred to him that she was the most unpredictable woman he'd ever met. 'It's impossible to understand you! You just don't behave the way every other woman would behave!'

'Given your views on women, I'll take that as a compliment.' Her eyes flickered around her and she licked her lips and moved closer to him, clearly unsettled by the sudden presence of the snake. 'I took a wrong turning.'

'A wrong turning?' His fingers bit into her upper arms and he gave her a little shake, incredulity mixing with exasperation. 'How could you possibly have taken a wrong turning? It isn't a complex route.'

Colour tinged her cheeks. 'I—I wasn't concentrating and I mixed up my left and my right.'

'You did what?' He shook his head, not even bothering to conceal his frustration with her. 'Out here, that sort of mistake can mean the difference between life and death. Don't you realise that? Are you stupid?' He felt her tense in his arms and then she pulled away from him and lifted her head to look at him.

Something shone in her eyes. Tears? Anger? He wasn't sure.

'Don't *ever* call me stupid.' Her voice was hoarse. Raw with hurt and pain. 'I accept that I took the wrong path and I realise that getting lost in the rainforest could have had disastrous consequences, but I'm *not* stupid. Don't call me that, ever again.'

He spread his hands, baffled as to why a single word should trigger a greater emotional response than an enormous snake. 'Then *why* did you allow yourself to get lost?'

She hesitated for a moment before answering, her chest rising and falling as she sucked the air into her lungs. 'Because I always confuse left and right.'

'Why would you confuse left and right?' He looked at her, uncomprehending, and she swallowed hard.

'Because I'm dyslexic.'

He stared at her. 'You're *dyslexic?*'

'That's right.'

Dyslexic? Rafael spent a moment or two sifting through the archives of his brain. 'You mean that you have problems reading?'

'Actually no, I'm not too bad at reading, but I'm hopeless at directions, I always mix up my left and right and I'm terrible at numbers.' She looked away from him, the heat burning in her cheeks. 'Absolutely appalling at numbers. But I suppose you already know that.'

He did?

Stunned by her confession and still trying to grasp the implications of her reluctant confession, he frowned. 'You didn't get lost yesterday on your way to the forest pool.'

'I asked Maria for directions and wrote left and right on my hands. It washed off in the pool, otherwise I wouldn't have got lost today.'

He let out a long breath. 'You're telling me that you can't read figures and yet you're running your own business?'

'It shouldn't matter. Plenty of dyslexics are extremely successful in business. My father is responsible for everything to do with the numbers. I can do everything else as long as I don't have to look at the figures. Figures confuse me.' Her tone was stiff and suddenly it all fell into place.

Not naïvety, not stupidity—*dyslexia.*

His expression suddenly grim, he reached down and closed a hand round her slender wrist. 'Come on.'

'Where are we going?'

'Back to the lodge, where I can ask you the questions that need to be asked. And this time I want the truth, Grace. No holding back.'

'My dyslexia isn't important and I don't want you to treat me differently because—'

'Grace—' he hauled her against him and glared down at her as anger, as intense as it was inexplicable, bubbled up inside him, 'do me a favour and let me decide what's important. This time I want to know everything. And I mean *everything*. If there's something in that head of yours that you don't think I need or want to know, then I *especially* want to know about that.'

Grace stood in his office again, listening to the interminable buzz of the phone. It was like an annoying insect, she thought numbly. He might be hiding out in the rainforest but people still didn't leave him alone.

Only he clearly had no intention of talking to anyone. He lifted the receiver, instructed someone to filter his calls until further notice, his tone short and clipped. Then he dropped the phone back into its cradle and turned his attention to her.

'All right.' He lounged in his chair, his eyes watchful. 'I'm listening.'

She straightened her shoulders. 'What do you want to know?'

'Everything.' His tone silky smooth, he leaned forward. 'I want to know *everything*, Grace. And don't leave anything out.'

She took a deep breath. 'I've already told you most of it. I had this idea for the coffee shop, and—'

'I'm not interested in your business. At this point in time I probably know more about your business than you do. I want to know about *you*. Go back further.' His eyes didn't shift from her face but his fingers drummed an impatient rhythm on the table. 'Back to your childhood. When did you realise that you were dyslexic?'

The breath hitched in her throat and she was suddenly swamped by feelings that she'd kept carefully hidden for years. 'It really isn't relevant, and—'

'Not relevant?' His fingers stilled and his voice was dangerously soft. 'Grace, someone is ripping off your business.'

She drew in a shaky breath. 'I know that.'

'And the reason they're able to rip off your business is clearly because they think you won't be any the wiser. You don't check the figures, do you?'

Mortified, she felt her face burn. It was like being back in a maths lesson, she thought miserably, when every other child was able to understand except her. 'No,' she said huskily, 'I don't check the figures. Not on the computer and not on paper.'

'So how do you know how the business is doing? How do you keep on top of what's happening with your business financially, if you can't make sense of the numbers?'

'Verbally. I just work with people that I trust and I rely on them to tell me what I need to know…' her voice tailed off and she shook her head as she realised the appalling naïvety of that statement '…or what they want me to know. It isn't the same thing, is it?'

His mouth tightened. 'It didn't occur to you that they might be taking advantage?'

She blinked several times to clear her vision. 'Why would it?'

He stared at her with naked exasperation. 'Because that's what people do, Grace. This is the real world and it's a harsh, unfriendly place. In the real world people lie and cheat and take advantage of each other.'

'Not all people,' she said quietly, forcing the words past the lump in her throat. 'There are plenty of people with good in them.'

'*Stop* being so generous.' He thumped his fist on the table and rose to his feet, visibly aggravated by her statement. 'That attitude is the reason that people were able to take advantage of you. You need to stop seeing good in everyone and toughen up. Otherwise you'll never succeed.'

The words were difficult to say but somehow she managed it. 'I haven't succeeded. I've lost money.'

'No. Someone else has done that for you.' He frowned. 'Your instincts told you that you should have been in profit, isn't that right?'

'I knew that the cafés were busy and that we were taking lots of money. I thought we should have been in profit, but our costs seemed high.'

'And you didn't question those figures?'

'No.'

'Well, I have,' he growled, raking his fingers through his hair and pacing across the room towards the huge glass window. 'I've spent all morning questioning those figures. Do you want to know the answers?'

Did she want to know? Her legs suddenly shook and the sickness rose in her stomach because she knew instinctively that what he was going to say wasn't going to be easy to hear. But since when had life been easy? When had she ever shied away from the hard and difficult? 'Of course I want to know the answers.' If wrong had been done then she wanted to put it right.

He turned to face her, his eyes dark, his hair gleaming blue-black in the strong light. 'Your father has been splitting the money with the dealer. Together they've driven up the price for the coffee while paying the bare minimum to Carlos and Filomena at the *fazenda*.'

Her father.

The sick feeling inside her intensified and she shook her head in an instinctive denial. 'There must be some mistake.' But even as she said the words she knew that there wasn't. And that knowledge tasted like poison in her mouth.

'It was your father.' His voice was brutally harsh, as if he was afraid that showing sympathy might somehow dilute the impact of his announcement. 'And that's not all.'

There was more?

What more could there possibly be?

How much deeper could the pain go?

Battling against a sense of bitter failure, she looked at him expectantly. 'Please go on,' she said quietly. 'Don't hold back.'

His mouth tightened. 'You mentioned that the refurbishment of the cafés cost more than you'd anticipated and I found out the reason for that, too. Your father agreed a cost with the builder that was far more than the going rate. Again, they split the difference. Are you following me?'

Oh, yes, she was following him.

She licked her lips. 'Go on.'

'Director's payments.' His voice was clipped and he thrust his hands in his pockets and paced again, this time back to his desk. 'Did they ever discuss those with you, Grace? Consultancy fees? Did you know about that figure?'

She nodded. 'My father told me that there were going to be some one-off payments to the consultant who did the design work for the new cafés. Did he overcharge?'

'To the tune of a quarter of a million pounds. Take all those figures together, and you have your profit. Except that someone took it out of the company and left you with a business that was just breaking even. They were clever enough not to let you go under because then they would have lost their source of income.' Rafael let out a long breath and picked up a set of papers from his desk. They were covered in circles and lines of red ink. 'Your father has stitched you up, Grace. He's the reason your business isn't in profit.'

Feeling faint and shaky, she nodded. 'Yes.'

'Why would he do that?'

'Oh,' she managed a smile, even though the effort was almost painful, 'I expect he was driven to it by having a daughter like me. I wasn't exactly a rewarding child to have around. I was never top in anything, you know, and I had two left feet when it came to sport. For a guy like my father, I must have been a bitter disappointment.' And it hurt. It still hurt.

'But he went into business with you.'

'Yes. At school I spent my whole time dreaming. I was full of ideas and I just knew I could do something good and useful with my life, even if I didn't take a conventional route. My father said he'd help me.' She turned away from him and walked to the window, staring into the rainforest without seeing anything. 'I suppose he saw a way of finally turning me from a disappointment to an advantage. I was never going to be able to check, was I?'

'So now what do you want to do?'

Scream? Cry? Thump someone? Slink into a deep hole and never emerge? 'I don't know. Let them know that I know.' She straightened her shoulders. 'I've basically been very stupid.'

'No.' His voice was fierce. 'You haven't been stupid. I see now that you have amazing vision and a huge capacity for hard work. The salary that you pay yourself is nothing.'

She frowned, not understanding the relevance of that statement. 'I wasn't ever interested in money, I've told you that.'

He inhaled sharply and dropped the papers on his desk. 'What were you interested in, Grace? Tell me.'

'Proving myself.' She wrapped her arms round her waist. 'I grew up with everyone telling me that I'd never make anything of myself. That I was never going to be anything or anyone.'

'Who told you that?'

'Everyone. My teachers. My father. Have you any idea how

it feels to be told that you're nothing? To be told that you'll never achieve anything?' She looked at him, her eyes lingering on the hard lines of his handsome face. Then she thought of the autocratic way he ran his business and realised that this man wouldn't have a clue what she was talking about. 'Never mind.'

'Why did they let you think you were nothing? Because of your dyslexia?' He frowned, his expression uncomprehending. 'Why was it such an issue? Why didn't they just help you? Schools are geared up to handle things like that these days.'

'Not mine.' She gave a laugh and turned away so that she didn't have to look at the question in his eyes. 'To start with they thought I was just naughty, unruly and stupid.' Stupid. Stupid. She tilted her head back and blinked back the tears. It always came back to that word. 'I hate talking about this.'

'Tough.' He stood up and paced towards her, his hands turning her to face him. 'This time you're going to keep talking until I've heard everything I need to hear.'

'Why do you need to hear any more?' Didn't he know enough?

His fingers tightened on her arms and he gave her a little shake. 'Talk.'

Why not? How much worse could she feel? 'At school I was slower than everyone else. The class idiot.' *She hated saying it and had to force herself to remember that he'd already formed his opinion of her.* 'The teachers used to be really impatient with me. My father—' She broke off and his mouth tightened.

'Your father?'

'It was difficult for him,' she said quietly, moving away from him and wrapping her arms around her waist in an unconscious gesture of comfort. 'He always wanted a son to follow him into business and what he got was a girl who couldn't even add up basic numbers.'

Rafael watched her. 'It didn't occur to him that you had a problem?'

'Oh, he knew I had a problem. He thought I was slow, lazy—' she chewed her lip '—stupid. Once or twice he tried to help me but I just couldn't understand him so he gave up.'

'So how were you diagnosed? What happened?' There was anger in his tone and Grace glanced at him miserably, knowing that he had reason to be angry.

She hadn't told him the truth about herself, had she?

She'd taken the loan without being entirely honest about her skills—*or lack of them.*

'A new teacher started at the school. She was much more progressive and had some experience with dyslexic students. She had her suspicions immediately and arranged for me to be tested. The results really shocked her. I was severely affected and she couldn't quite believe that no one had helped me before.' Grace shrugged. 'She saved my life. She spent hours with me, hours of her own time, helping me. And she taught me ways of coping. She showed me all the things that I could do really well and she taught me that I wasn't stupid. But most of all she taught me never to give up.'

Rafael ran a hand over the back of his neck and closed his eyes briefly. 'And you didn't think this was worth mentioning to me before?'

'You only gave me ten minutes.' Her pathetic attempt at a joke fell flat under his stare and she sighed. 'No, because I've never made excuses for myself. And I just wanted to live my life by the same rules as everyone else.'

'You didn't mention it when you were given the loan?'

'If I'd told you then you wouldn't have given me the loan.'

He frowned. 'That's not true.'

'Yes, it is true. You would have said that I wasn't the sort of person to be running a business—' she swallowed painfully '—and you would have been right. I see that now. I thought I could run a business providing I had people to help me, but if you can't trust your own family, who can you trust?'

'That is a question that I'm not qualified to answer because in my experience no one is to be trusted, least of all family.'

'Oh.' She gave a painful smile. 'Does your family lie and cheat and try and rip you off? It's enough to shatter all your illusions, isn't it?'

'I don't have a family, Grace,' a muscle worked in his lean, aggressive jaw and the sudden flicker in his eyes discouraged any further questioning on that subject, 'and nor do I have any illusions about people.'

'Well, that makes you the sensible one, doesn't it?' She let out a long breath and studied the floor, wondering where to go from here. 'Look, I'm very grateful to you for trying to sort out the mess and find out what is going on. It's more than I managed to do. And you must be very angry with me.'

'You're right that I'm angry.' He prowled across the room towards her, his tempestuous mood sizzling the air around them. 'I'm livid.'

'Yes.' She forced herself to face his anger even though her knees shook and her palms were damp. 'You have every right to be angry. I lost Filomena and Carlos a significant amount of money.'

His dark brows met in a frown. 'That isn't why I'm angry. Obviously I intend to give them all the money they need, although I'll have to be subtle because they're very proud. No, I'm angry because you didn't give me all the information. I'm angry because you didn't tell me any of this sooner.'

'But I *did* tell you that I hadn't stolen money,' she muttered in a feeble attempt at self-defence but the words subsided in her throat as he delivered her a furious glare that told her everything she needed to know about the current state of his *extremely* volatile temperament.

'Given that you withheld the one vital piece of information that would have actually allowed me to believe you, you'll agree that the evidence wasn't exactly stacked in your favour?'

She chewed her lip. 'I suppose I just expected you to trust me.'

'And why would I do a thing like that?' His voice was soft and he moved close to her, something dangerous lighting his dark eyes. 'I'm not like you, Grace. I don't trust people I don't know. I don't trust the people I *do* know. The truth is that I don't trust anyone at all, and especially not when all the evidence points to guilt. I don't give people the benefit of the doubt. Haven't you heard that about me?' The atmosphere throbbed with suppressed emotion. His anger, her misery and something far, far more powerful than either.

Sexual chemistry. It simmered between them, providing an undercurrent that heated the atmosphere.

'I heard that about you,' she said hoarsely, struggling to ignore the sudden rush of heat that engulfed her body. 'It's hard not to. The papers are full of what a bad boy you are.'

A humourless smile touched his firm mouth. 'And yet, even knowing that about me, you chose to fly all the way out here to try and persuade me to extend your loan.' He was standing close to her now. *Incredibly* close. 'You must have known I'd ask you difficult questions involving numbers.'

She gave a wan smile. 'I just hoped they'd be questions that I'd memorised the answers to.'

He shook his head and raked his fingers through his hair. 'Senior businessmen with decades of experience think twice before discussing numbers with me and yet you walked into the lion's den like a baby deer offering itself up as a sacrifice.'

Her heart bumping against her chest, she shook her head. 'No,' she said breathlessly, 'I didn't do that. I knew from the first moment I saw you that there was good in you. I knew that the papers were lying.'

He stepped back from her and she sensed his immediate withdrawal. She sensed the depth of his cynicism and something close to distaste.

'Don't do that, Grace.' His voice was rough, almost aggressive, as if he were determined to keep her at a distance, and perhaps he was because he turned away, leaving her only a glimpse of the hard lines of his profile. 'Don't give me virtues that don't exist. Don't trust in people that don't deserve your trust. You made that mistake with your father and his little band of accomplices. And you made it with me.'

'No.'

'Yes.' His tone was savage and when he turned to face her again his eyes blazed dark. 'You made that mistake with me, last night.'

It was the first reference to the night of stormy passion and she felt her whole body heat at the memory. 'I don't consider last night to be a mistake.'

'No?' He looked at her then, his dark eyes hard and his mouth set as he forced her to confront the truth. 'And yet you didn't hear the words you wanted to hear, did you? You didn't hear love or gentleness. You didn't hear promises or talk of a future together. Last night was all about sex, Grace. Hot, primitive sex. Are you willing to admit that?'

Her heart was hammering against her chest. 'Yes.' What other answer could she give? She wasn't going to admit it was about love, was she? Even she didn't understand these feelings that had rushed up and engulfed her. How could she expect him to—this man who didn't even think that such things as love existed? *This man who was so damaged that he expected the worst from every woman he met.*

He stepped closer to her and this time his arms gripped hers as if he wanted to be completely sure that she was paying attention. 'I thought you were guilty, Grace. I thought you were guilty as hell, but I didn't even care because all I was interested in was your body under mine and your unquestioning surrender.'

And that was what she'd given him, of course. Her unquestioning surrender. She'd given him everything he'd demanded from her.

She didn't flinch under his gaze. 'Are you trying to shock me?'

'No.' His fingers bit into the soft flesh of her arms. 'I'm trying to remind you who I am so that there's no mistake.'

'There's no mistake, Rafael.' Grace said the words softly. 'It's true that I've made mistakes but last night wasn't one of them.'

'You're deluding yourself.'

'No.' And she wasn't. Even if he sent her home within the hour, she'd have no regrets about what they'd shared. How could she, when the night they'd spent together was the closest to perfect that her life had ever become? And suddenly the heat pulsing between them and the wicked pull of temptation drew her onto her toes and she dragged her lips over the roughness of his jaw.

'No.' He tried to step back from her but she slid her arms round his neck and pressed her body against the hardness of his.

'I want you, Rafael.' She whispered the words against the warmth of his neck, feeling the strength and power of his shoulders under her seeking hands. 'If last night was a mistake, then it was a mistake that I intend to repeat.'

With a soft curse he curled his fingers round both her wrists, clearly intending to remove her arms from his neck, but then he seemed to think better of it, his hands sliding down her body and settling in the centre of her back. 'A better man than I would probably stop you, but I'm not that man.' He hauled her roughly against him and there was a fire in his eyes hot enough to burn both of them. Suddenly she found that she could hardly breathe.

'I'm glad you're not that man.'

His mouth hovered tantalisingly close to hers. 'I'm *not* a good person.'

'You're the only person I want.' And she wanted him now. She wanted him so badly that she was afraid her entire body might melt under the intense heat of her sexual longing. 'Can't you feel it?'

He hesitated for a moment longer and then, with a low growl, he brought his mouth down on hers.

Intoxicating excitement immediately engulfed her and she clutched at his shoulders, knowing that without the support of his firm hands holding her she would certainly fall.

He drove her backwards with his powerful frame, until she felt the edge of his desk pressing against the backs of her thighs.

In a decisive movement he lifted her, pushing her thighs apart and then sliding his hands over the curve of her bottom with a groan of masculine appreciation. His mouth devoured hers and he yanked her against him so that her soft feminine core was pressed against the hard ridge of his manhood.

Shockingly aroused and unaware of anything except the touch of his hands and the erotic slide of his tongue in her mouth, she reached for his shirt, ripping at the buttons in her attempt to get closer to him. His shirt fell open and her fingers encountered silky male chest hair and hard male muscle.

And then his hand was between her thighs, and his clever, seeking fingers dispensed with the totally inadequate barrier of her panties and slid into the hot, moist warmth that awaited him.

Grace felt her body explode in an instantaneous reaction that was as shocking as it was powerful and she cried out his name as her body pulsed around the determined stroke of his fingers. But somehow that glorious release didn't give her the satisfaction that her body craved and she moaned in desperation, her trembling hands reaching urgently for the zip of his trousers.

Without lifting his mouth from hers, he covered her hand with his, speeding the task, and she gave a soft whimper as she felt the velvety brush of his arousal against her inner thigh.

He pushed up her thighs, positioned her to his satisfaction and then thrust hard into her sweet, welcoming warmth.

Excitement rocketed to unbearable proportions and he drove into her again and again with almost explosive force. She strained against him, completely swept away by his primal possession, *his ferocious sexual hunger,* and then her body erupted in a climax so intense that for a moment she lost all sense of time.

As the world splintered around her, she heard him mutter something harsh against her neck, felt his hands anchoring her hips, and then he powered into her for a final time, his fingers digging hard into the curve of her bottom as he reached his own completion and his body emptied itself into hers.

CHAPTER NINE

SHATTERED and stunned, Rafael steadied his breathing and gradually became aware of his surroundings. His face was still buried in her neck and the sweet, tempting scent of her hair and skin teased his senses and created a dull haze over his usually acute brain.

Forced to acknowledge that he couldn't concentrate on anything at all when she was this close, he reluctantly moved his hands from her hips.

Without his hands supporting her she flopped forward, her head against his chest, her blonde hair soft and tangled. Her breathing was unsteady and she rubbed her fingers over his chest and gently pressed her lips to his skin.

The affectionate gesture took him by surprise and for endless seconds Rafael stood still, his hands suspended in the air while he decided what to do with them. What he *wanted* to do was to drag her back into his arms and just hug her, and the impulse shocked and spooked him because he'd never before felt a desire to express affection following sex.

Reminding himself that gestures of affection could easily be misconstrued, he gritted his teeth and let his hands fall to his sides. So far he'd been entirely honest with her, and that wasn't going to change.

But something *had* changed, hadn't it?

Since when had he ever been tempted to have sex with a woman on his desk in his glass office?

No one would have described the encounter as romantic. Hot, yes. Sizzling, yes. Incredibly powerful, definitely. But it had been a primitive act of lust that had bordered on the sordid and if there was one thing that Grace Thacker definitely didn't deserve, it was sordid.

Gritting his teeth to resist the temptation to sample her for a second time, Rafael gently eased away from her and made some rapid adjustments to their clothing.

For a moment she didn't speak. And then she slid off the desk cautiously, as if she wasn't entirely sure that her legs were going to support her.

'There are things we need to sort out.' His voice was rough and he thought he saw her flinch slightly when she lifted her head to look at him.

'Absolutely.' Her voice was unsteady and her smile was a little too bright. 'I should be going.'

'Going?' His dark brows met in a frown. 'Going where?'

'Home, of course.' She slipped her feet into her shoes, which had somehow become dislodged from her feet during their frantic encounter. 'I have things to work out. And you need to get on with your life.'

He stared at her with blank incredulity. 'That's it? We have phenomenal sex and you just walk out on me?'

She smoothed her dress with hands that shook. 'I thought that was what you wanted, Rafael. No commitment.'

In the grip of an escalating tension that he didn't entirely understand, Rafael strode across to her. 'There's no way I'm letting you go,' her look of astonishment matched his own feelings and he quickly added, 'yet. I mean, I'm not letting you go, yet.' Eventually, yes, of course.

Her eyes lingered on his mouth and then she looked away. 'I have to go home. You know I do. I have a million things to sort out.'

'What things?' *What could possibly take priority over him?*

'How can you ask me that? My life is in crisis. My business is going under and my own father has cheated me. I need to confront him about it and then I need to find someone to help me make sense of the figures…' The dark shadows under her eyes and the unmistakable shake in her voice racked his already soaring tension levels several notches higher. Surveying her slim, delicate frame, he felt a burst of almost volcanic anger at her father for causing her pain.

'You're not dealing with this on your own.'

'It's fine. Really. I'm tougher than I look.'

His eyes raked her pale features with no small degree of irony. 'I sincerely hope so,' he said with sardonic bite, 'because you look as though you'd be blown over by a small gust of wind. If I hadn't actually seen you in action in the jungle I'd think that you were fragile.'

'I'm not fragile, Rafael. I think I've proved that to you.' Her eyes met his boldly and he knew that she was remembering the rampant, almost aggressive nature of their last steamy encounter.

For a brief, disconcerting moment he wondered whether he'd hurt her but the look shimmering in her blue eyes assured him of the opposite and, remembering her soft cries, urging him on, he knew that she'd been as desperate as him.

'Maybe *not* fragile, but how do you intend to deal with your father?'

'I don't know yet. I have a long flight ahead. That should give me time to think about it.'

He frowned. 'You have no idea who in your company you can trust.'

'That's right.' She gave a shrug. 'I'll just have to develop a suspicious nature as fast as possible.'

'We both know you don't have a suspicious bone in your body. You trust *everyone*,' Rafael growled, just *appalled* by the thought that someone else might still take advantage of her. Driven as he was by emotions that he didn't even bother trying to understand, it suddenly became imperative that she stayed, but she was shaking her head.

'This time I'll employ a stranger. Someone with good references.'

The thought of a total stranger sitting across a desk from her, giving her advice that might be completely useless, made him cold. 'I'll do it.'

'Sorry?'

'Stay here with me and I'll help you with your finances. I don't know why I didn't think of it before. It's the perfect solution.' Satisfied that he was now back in control, he was more than a little disconcerted to see her shake her head again.

'No. Definitely not. I don't need your help.'

He looked at her with naked incredulity. 'You're refusing me?'

She flushed slightly. 'I can do it by myself. I don't need your help.'

'Offhand I can't think of anyone who needs it more.'

She lifted her chin and he saw the flash of determination in her eyes. 'I need to do it by myself. I should do it by myself. And anyway, why would you be able to do a better job than me?'

'Because I have extensive experience with liars and cheats and you have none,' he slotted in helpfully, wondering why they were even having this conversation. 'It's perfectly obvious that I should help you.'

'It's not obvious to me.' There was a stubborn note in his voice and he decided that perhaps she simply hadn't understood him correctly.

'Let me just spell out what I'm trying to say here. I'm pro-
posing to give you all the money you could possibly need to
keep your business solvent, straighten up your accounts and
then appoint someone from my team to look after your finances
from now on.'

'That's very generous of you.'

Confident that he was now in familiar territory, he smiled.
'It's the least I can do.'

'But I don't want you to do it.'

The smile froze on his face. 'You don't?'

'No.' She frowned thoughtfully. 'Well, actually I'd be silly
to turn down the offer of someone from your team to help me
in the future because at least then I know that I have someone
I can trust, so yes to that, thank you, but I don't want anything
else from you.'

'I'm offering you money.'

'I know. I don't want your money. And I'm sure you have
better things to do with your time than help me understand the
figures. You'd find it horribly frustrating.'

Never having encountered a woman who didn't want money
from him, Rafael found himself at a loss. 'I *want* to help you,'
he said quickly, surprised to find that he actually did. He
couldn't stand the thought of anyone taking advantage of her.
'In order to shift your father from the business you're going to
need your facts straight.'

'Yes, that's true.' She bit her lip and looked at him. 'You'd help
me with the figures? Really? But you must be horribly busy with
your own business. You're always glued to your computer screen.'

'My work isn't particularly demanding at the moment,' he
lied swiftly, 'so I'd be more than happy to go through your
accounts with you.' And he'd make sure that she took his
money, too, although he was prepared to postpone the inevitable argument about that subject.

'I'm infuriating to teach. I'm terrible with numbers.'

Unable to conceive of a single situation in which he'd find her infuriating, Rafael shrugged dismissively. 'I'm brilliant with numbers, so that's fine. Although you'll have to tell me the best way to go through them so that you understand what I'm saying.'

'Oh.' Her cheeks were pink. 'My father never cared whether I understood or not. He just told me the figures.'

'And they were the *wrong* ones.' Resisting the temptation to punch his fist through something to relieve his mounting tension, Rafael urged her towards the table that only moments earlier had been the scene of their passionate encounter. 'Sit down. I'm going to teach you to handle numbers.'

She hesitated. 'My flight leaves Rio in four hours.'

'You won't be on it,' he informed her immediately. 'I don't want you to leave.'

She gave a faint smile. 'Because the sex between us is so amazing?'

Her honesty surprised him. 'That's one reason, yes,' Rafael replied with an equal amount of honesty. 'But I also don't want to see your father get away with stripping money from your company.'

'No.' Her eyes lingered on his, warm and admiring. 'Of course you don't. You care a great deal about Carlos and Filomena.'

Rafael found himself so captivated by the look of approval in her amazing blue eyes that for a moment he didn't answer. 'Yes,' he said finally. 'Carlos and Filomena.'

'You really love them and they love you, too, I could see that instantly. I'm so sorry they've been hurt because of me.' There was a choked note to her voice that halted the instinctive denial that her mention of love had brought rushing to his lips.

She wasn't going to cry, was she?

So far she held the record for being the only female never to resort to feminine tantrums while in his company.

And, considering everything she'd been through in the past forty-eight hours, he was more and more astonished by her composure.

'I'm very fond of them, that's certainly true, and you don't need to worry about it any more because it will all be sorted out,' he told her hastily. 'And when it's time to leave you can use one of my private jets.' But as he focused on the tiny dimple that played alongside the corner of her mouth, he promised himself that it wasn't going to be any time soon.

'It's incredibly kind of you to help me.'

'*Not* kind,' he said immediately, frowning slightly as he corrected her altogether inaccurate description of him. 'I have all sorts of thoroughly selfish reasons for keeping you here.'

'Like sex?' The sudden flare of heat in her eyes astonished him.

'That's certainly part of it.'

She gave a soft smile. 'Yes. The sex is pretty amazing.'

Stunned by her direct approach, and feeling an uncomfortable flare of lust, Rafael ran his fingers through his hair. 'Let's get on with these numbers while I'm still able to concentrate.'

Three hours later Grace sat back in her chair and let out a long breath. 'Well.' She smiled at him. 'You're right about one thing. You *are* brilliant at numbers. And you're brilliant at teaching.'

For the first time in her life after a session on finance, her head wasn't bursting and her brain wasn't twisting itself into knots. Nor did she feel like a complete failure.

Rafael put down the red pen he'd been using to illustrate a certain point. 'I can see how hard it is for you and that makes the whole thing even more amazing.'

'What's amazing?'

He shook his head and leaned back in his chair. His hair gleamed blue-black in the late-evening sun and the usual chill in his eyes had been replaced by something significantly warmer. 'The fact that you've managed to run a successful business despite your problems with numbers. I'm staggered. And impressed.'

'How can you say that? I didn't make you a profit and, because of me, Carlos and Filomena lost money.'

The chill was back in his eyes. '*Not* because of you, but the people around you.' The dark frown cleared from his brow. 'But that's history. From now on your advisors are going to be hand-picked by me.' He glanced back at her company accounts and flicked through the pages with a disbelieving shake of his head. 'Your takings in the cafés are amazing. If your father hadn't been draining the money away you would have had a hugely profitable business.'

She couldn't resist teasing him. 'Would I have made you rich?'

He glanced up, a strange expression on his handsome face. 'If I had more people like you working for me then my life would be a great deal simpler, *meu amorzinho*. How do you manage to keep the cafés so busy?'

She shrugged. 'I'm good at ideas. I'm hopeless at financial detail and probably always will be, but I see the bigger picture. I know what people want and what is likely to work. I was good at pulling in the customers.'

'Don't put it in the past tense.' He dropped the accounts onto the table and looked at her thoughtfully. 'How would you feel about extending Café Brazil?'

Her eyes widened. 'You mean across the country?'

'Actually I meant across the world,' he said drily, the faint smile that touched his mouth telling her how amused he was by her provincial ambitions. 'I think it's an idea that could become a global phenomenon.'

'There are already lots of very successful chains of coffee shops.'

'True, but none of them have you at the helm. You have an astonishing flare for innovation.'

She couldn't prevent the warm glow of happiness that suddenly filled her. 'You've just spent hours going through numbers with me and yet you still make me sound like an asset, not a hindrance.'

He looked at her with ill-concealed impatience. 'You *are* an asset. Forget the numbers. Adding up the numbers is the easy bit—anyone trained in accountancy can do that.' The dismissive wave of his hand told her everything she needed to know on his opinion of accountants. 'The hard bit is coming up with the business idea and making it work. Making it original. And you've done that.'

'But I'm very hands-on. I mean,' she bit her lip, trying not to be daunted by the fact that she was discussing her small business with a billionaire who made more money in an hour than she would in a lifetime, 'I know everyone working in all the cafés and we all meet up regularly. I can't imagine handling anything bigger.'

'And if you turned your business into a global enterprise then you wouldn't have time to linger in the rainforest with me.' He gave her a wolfish smile and she felt her heart perform a frantic dance in her chest. 'No, *meu amorzinho,* you're right. That's not a good plan. If we go global, then I'll do it for you.'

'I think I ought to concentrate on sorting out the mess I've made of the business I've got,' she croaked, 'without taking on any more responsibility.'

'There is no mess and it is sorted out. The dealer is no longer in business.'

'Seriously?' Grace was visibly startled by that piece of information, her eyes widening. 'How can you be sure?'

'Because I'm the one who helped persuade him that seeking an alternative form of employment as an immediate priority

would be advisable for his general health,' Rafael drawled, his
tone leaving her with the distinct impression that the dealer was
probably now an *extremely* unhappy man.

'Which just leaves my father.'

'Indeed.' Rafael sat back in his chair. 'I still have to deal with
him, but everything else is sorted out. The guy now in charge
of your finances is clever and approachable. You can ask him
anything. And if he shoots one impatient glance in your direction then tell me and I will fire him.'

Touched by the sentiment behind his characteristically
arrogant statement, she smiled. 'Thank you.'

'He'll sort out the purchase of your coffee.'

'I had a couple of ideas about that.'

'Go on.'

'I want to stop going through a third party and deal directly
with Carlos and Filomena at the *fazenda,* so that the money
goes directly to them. I'm going to deal with them myself so
that I build a relationship. That way, if there are any problems
with production then I'm the first to know and if they have any
concerns with the way I'm doing business, they can tell me.'

'All right.'

Suddenly horribly self-conscious and not really understanding why, she stood up and paced across the room. 'I'm going
to donate a percentage of our profits to a charity protecting the
rainforest. I know that means lowering our profit,' she said
quickly, 'but the move isn't entirely altruistic. These days many
consumers have a conscience so I think they'll like the idea that
the coffee they drink supports the rainforest. And perhaps we
can use our photo boards to show them exactly what their
money is supporting.'

There was a long silence. 'Why do you always walk around
when you're nervous? You did it on that first day when you were
trying to persuade me to extend your loan.'

'I just find sitting still too stressful. Maybe it reminds me of school. So what do you think?'

'About your charity donation?' He gave a tolerant smile. 'I think you'll never be a billionaire if you're prepared to throw away money so flagrantly but that doesn't matter because I have enough money for both of us.'

Her smile faded. 'I don't want your money.'

'I'm starting to realise that.' He leaned forward, a hint of wry humour in his eyes. 'You're the first woman who has never expected me to give her anything.'

'You've given me loads,' she muttered. 'You've sat and helped me understand numbers, which is something that no one else has ever bothered to do. You were amazingly patient with me and you went over it again and again without once sounding irritated or annoyed. And you've sorted out the dealer for me and I would have *hated* doing that because it's so easy for people to tie me in knots.'

'I was talking about money.'

'Yes.' She gave a slight frown. 'Well, money isn't always what's important, is it?'

'Maybe not. You're a very unusual woman.' His lingering gaze unsettled her and she moved from one foot to the other.

'You mean because I can't add up?'

'No, I *don't* mean that.' He rose to his feet and strode across to her, laughter in his eyes. 'I really couldn't care less whether you can add up and I've had enough of talking about your business, numbers and your father. We've just about got time for a swim before Maria serves dinner.'

They walked down the path and Grace stopped as she saw the bright red ribbon tied to the trees. 'What are those for?'

'You,' Rafael said gruffly, urging her along. 'I instructed my staff to mark the path to the pool so that there's no chance you can get lost again. You follow the ribbons.'

The lump built in her throat. 'You did that for me?'

He looked at her for a moment and then shrugged. 'It seemed less trouble than tracking you through the rainforest.'

But even his casual answer wasn't enough to dampen the happiness inside her. He'd thought about what she needed. *About what might help her.*

The pool was deliciously cool and refreshing and Grace slid into the water with an appreciative moan. 'I wish I could transport this pool back to London with me.'

'Why would you need to do that?' In a series of swift movements, Rafael removed all his clothes and stood for a moment, watching her, completely unselfconscious.

Confronted by such a blatant display of potent masculinity, she felt her cheeks heat. 'Because I love it.'

'Then stay in the rainforest.' With a shrug that indicated that he considered the problem solved, Rafael plunged head first into the water in a smooth, athletic dive.

She gave a gasp of shock as he surfaced right next to her. There was a dangerous glint in his eyes.

'There are all sorts of potentially lethal predators in this pool, *minha paixao,*' he said huskily, sliding his hand behind her back and urging her against his hard, powerful body. 'You need to be careful.'

Engulfed by a sexual excitement that shocked her, she pushed against him and lifted her mouth to his. 'Is that right?'

It was crazy to allow herself to become this involved with him, but how could she stop herself? It was as if her mind and her body were outside her control and she gave a low moan of encouragement as she felt his hands slide down her body, removing her costume in the process. In a matter of seconds she was naked but she didn't even care because all she could think about was what he did to her.

'Rafael…' She moaned his name against the slick muscle

of his shoulder and felt the hot, hard throb of his arousal brush against her.

He clamped a hand behind her head and captured her mouth, his tongue creating an explosion of sensations that sent her whole body into meltdown.

She wriggled and writhed against him in an attempt to get closer still, her body slippery and lithe in the water, and she heard him mutter something in Portuguese and then he held her firmly and entered her with a smooth, sliding thrust.

The contrast between the cool of the pool and the incredible, pulsing heat of his body made her cry out and her head fell backwards, her hair trailing in the water as he thrust into her with a rhythm so exquisitely perfect that she almost immediately lost control. Her body exploded around his and she heard his answering groan and felt the sudden increase in masculine thrust that heralded his own completion.

Drained, sated and more than a little dazed, Grace closed her eyes and clung to his wide shoulders, relieved that he was still holding her, otherwise she had a strong suspicion that she would have drowned and died happy.

'*Not* leaving Brazil any time soon,' he purred, stroking her damp hair away from her face with a gentle hand.

Barely able to focus, she opened her eyes and looked at him. Did he care about her? Surely he *had* to care in order to respond like that? And he'd changed towards her, she felt it. He'd softened in his attitude. They shared a bond that wasn't just sexual.

Did they, just possibly, have some sort of future?

Watching Grace sip cautiously at a glass of wine, Rafael wondered why it was that everything about her fascinated him.

And why, he wondered with a faint frown, had repeated sex done nothing to dampen his ravenous libido?

He was rapidly coming to the conclusion that he just might be addicted to Grace Thacker's incredibly lithe, seductive body.

He noticed the faint shadows under her eyes with a frown. 'You're tired?'

'A little.' She put her glass down and picked up her fork, taking a small mouthful of the dish that Maria had put in front of her. 'More worried than tired, if I'm honest.'

'Worried?' Discovering that he absolutely didn't want her to feel worried, Rafael leaned forward. 'What's worrying you? Tell me and I'll solve the problem.'

'My father.'

'I'll deal with him.'

'I don't want you to. It isn't your problem. And it isn't the thought of dealing with him that bothers me. It's everything else.' She toyed with her food. 'I suppose I'm just very upset.'

'Why? Your business is going to be fine.'

'But it isn't just about the business, is it?'

'Isn't it?' Rafael stared at her blankly, trying to see what he'd missed, and she gave a twisted smile.

'This is going to sound really crazy but I feel as though I've lost my father.' She swallowed. 'And I know it's mad to feel that way because obviously he's never cared about me but that's a really hard thing to accept. I've spent my entire life trying to please him and make him proud of me but it's obvious that my father didn't ever want me to succeed. That's pretty hard to take.'

'Why?' He frowned at her. 'That says everything about your father and nothing about you.'

'I know that's the theory,' she said in a small voice, poking at the food on her plate, 'but it isn't that easy in practise.'

Rafael sighed. 'Having children is a massive responsibility which the majority of people get hideously wrong,' he said in his usual cynical drawl. 'Which just goes to show that you should never put your faith in people. Better to rely on yourself.'

'And I do. I always have done.' Her eyes slid away from his. 'But what sort of life is it, without love?'

'A simple one?' Seriously disconcerted by the direction of the conversation, Rafael reached across the table and piled some food on her plate, noting that she didn't eat anywhere near enough. 'Forget it, now. You need to toughen up and learn to be less trusting.'

'Don't give me any more…' she held up a hand to stop him filling her plate '…I'm not really hungry. And I'm not sure that I really want to toughen up. I don't really want to live the sort of life where I don't feel anything.'

'Believe me, it's much simpler that way,' Rafael assured her and she lifted her eyes to his.

'Did she really hurt you? Your ex-wife?'

Everything about him tensed in an instinctive rejection of her intimate question but then he told himself that a short reminder of other people's failings might help her build that shell she so badly needed. 'No. She didn't hurt me.' *It was a long time since he'd let a woman hurt him but he had no intention of revealing that much about himself.*

'Were you in love with her?'

Sliding his mind back into the present, he raised an eyebrow in silent mockery. 'What do you think?'

'Well, I know you claim not to believe in love, but you *did* marry her. And your reputation is for avoiding commitment so there must have been a reason.'

'There was a reason.' Emotion, dark and deadly, rushed towards him and he forced it away. 'She told me that she was pregnant.'

'Oh.' She put her fork down on her plate. 'You married her for that reason?'

'Yes.'

'And what happened? Or would you rather not talk about it?

I mean, I know you don't have a child so…' she hesitated, stumbling over the words, clearly anxious to protect his feelings '…if it makes you sad then let's change the subject. I'm so sorry. I should never have asked.'

'I'm not sitting here pining, Grace.' His tone was rougher than he'd intended. 'There was no baby.'

Her eyes misted. 'She lost it?'

He studied her with a mixture of disbelief and fascination. Her emotions were so incredibly close to the surface. Everything she felt was reflected on her face. She was designed to go through life being severely bruised.

'There was never a baby to lose.' His tone was harsher than he intended and his knuckles whitened on his wine glass. Forcing himself to slacken his grip, he studied her shocked face with a faint smile. 'So you see, Grace Thacker, even the most cynical of us can be duped.'

'She *lied* to you in order to persuade you to marry her?' Her eyes were bright with sympathy and something much, much softer that flowed over his ragged nerve-endings and soothed like a balm. 'She loved you *that much?*'

Rapidly coming to the conclusion that Grace Thacker's mind worked in a completely different way from the rest of the population's, Rafael felt his muscles clench. 'She didn't love me at all.'

'But if she—'

'Being married to a billionaire comes with certain compensations,' Rafael drawled lightly, resigning himself to the reality of pointing out what, to him, was totally obvious, 'not least of all a guaranteed income for life.'

'You think she married you for your money?'

'I *know* that she married me for my money.' He watched her across the table. *Was she really that naïve?* 'What else?'

'Is that all you think you have to offer a woman? Money?'

She sounded genuinely shocked and he heard the bitterness in his laugh.

'No. Apparently I excel in the bedroom, as well.' He watched as the colour bloomed in her cheeks. 'After I ended the relationship and gave her the settlement she'd worked so hard for, she was keen to make it really clear that she was more than prepared to continue with that element of our relationship. *After* she'd sold her story to the tabloids, of course.'

'She talked to the papers—'

'They *all* talk to the papers,' Rafael said, not even bothering to keep the bitterness out of his tone. 'It's another lucrative source of income for my ex-girlfriends and my ex-wife. I suppose you could call it lateral thinking. Once they've finished fleecing me in person, they carry on milking the relationship in print.'

There was a moment of silence and then she put her fork down, apparently giving up on her food. 'Well—' her tone was deceptively light '—your ex-wife sounds like a very special person. Perhaps we should introduce her to my father. At least they'd understand each other. But that was just one relationship, Rafael. Haven't you ever been tempted to try again?'

'Marriage, no. Sex—' he raised his glass towards her '—yes. Quite frequently actually.'

She blushed sweetly. 'Well, I know that you've been very busy in that department, according to the papers, anyway. But I wasn't really talking about sex or marriage. I was talking about love.'

'Don't talk to me about love, Grace. Don't ever talk to me about love.' He watched her flinch. 'All relationships are based on mutual greed. One person has what another person wants.'

'Not everyone is like your ex-wife.'

'The world is full of people like my ex-wife.'

'Do you truly believe that?' Her voice was suddenly spirited and her eyes flashed with something that came close to annoyance. 'You're an incredibly intelligent man. Are you really going to let a few greedy girlfriends ruin your view of women?'

Not just a few greedy girlfriends.

Something dark and uncomfortable churned inside him and he tensed as he was forced to contemplate the murky depths of his soul that he so rigorously ignored.

Finding himself on the receiving end of her faintly accusing blue gaze, he was suddenly tempted to reveal all those things about himself that he kept hidden, just to reinstate himself in her good books. Shaken by the powerful and uncharacteristic urge to confide when confiding was as alien to him as running a business by consensus, he clamped his mouth shut.

And why did he care what she thought of him when the good opinion of others was a matter of complete indifference to him?

He suddenly realised that she was staring at him again and something powerful throbbed between them. Refusing to be drawn into something more than physical intimacy, he gave a faint smile.

'What was the question again? Am I going to let a few greedy girlfriends affect my view of the whole human race? The answer is yes, Grace.' He raised his glass in her direction, unable to keep the mockery out of his gaze. 'I think I probably am. And don't feel sorry for me because I'm as bad as they are. I keep women around for as long as they're useful to me. Perhaps you'd better remember that and run while you can.'

Her lips parted and he saw her breathing quicken. 'I'm not running anywhere. And I think you're completely wrong about who you are. There's so much more to you than that.'

She was such a ridiculous optimist, he thought savagely, and it was no wonder she'd been so hurt in her life when she laboured so hard to find good in people.

'No, Grace, there isn't. Why do you think I choose to spend a large amount of my time in the rainforest?'

'Well it's very beautiful and if I had a place like this I'd never go near a city—' She broke off and sighed. 'I'm *trying* to understand you…'

And she would try, of course, because Grace Thacker was a woman who had to get under everyone's skin. 'I don't require you to understand me. I thought I'd made that clear.'

'But I do understand, well, part of it, at least. You've never met anyone who just wanted you for yourself. For who you are. And I know the feeling because I haven't either. Not that I exactly worry about someone wanting me for my money…' she let out a long breath and smiled. 'I suppose it's easier for me.'

'It's easy for me too,' he said softly, watching her face. 'I just set my expectations accordingly. And you need to do the same. Just use people for what they can give you.'

She hesitated for a moment and then she straightened her shoulders. 'I can't do that. No matter what happens in life, you can't really change the person you are, can you? All my life I've wanted to be loved the way I am. All my life I struggled to please people—my teachers, my father—but it never worked. I've just disappointed people. They get impatient and frustrated with me. Do you want to know something funny?'

Hating the thought that they'd all made her life so unhappy and finding the whole conversation just about as far from amusing as it was possible to get, Rafael frowned. 'What?'

'You think you're such a hard, bad person but you're the first and only person who has ever taken the time to go through numbers with me without getting horribly impatient. You spent a whole afternoon teaching maths to someone who just doesn't get it and not once did you drum your fingers on the table, glare at me or tug at your hair. So stop pretending that you're just this cold, ruthless money-making machine.'

Startled by her interpretation of his actions, Rafael

thought for a moment. 'I need you to understand the figures. It's the only way you'll be able to have a conversation with your father.'

'Right. Well, you did it in a very nice way, so thank you. You're a good and patient teacher.'

A good and patient teacher? Wondering what his staff would make of that entirely inaccurate assessment of his qualities, Rafael ran a hand over the back of his neck, suddenly determined to make sure that she knew exactly who she was. 'You're making a mistake, Grace. I *am* a cold, ruthless money-making machine.'

'No. You're nothing like that. You have great humanity but you don't even recognise it yourself any more, because you've spent your life with people attached to you like leeches, wanting something from you.'

Wondering why he was still sitting opposite her when the conversation topic was so hugely distant from his comfort zone, Rafael tapped his fingers on the table. 'You're talking nonsense because you're upset about your father.'

'Maybe. And it's time I faced up to what needs to be done. Will you arrange for your plane to fly me back to London tomorrow?'

Appalled at the prospect of her leaving, Rafael frowned. 'I need to be in London in two weeks' time on business; you can come with me then. We'll see your father together.'

'No.' She shook her head. 'This is something that I need to do by myself. And I have to do it now. I don't want to wait any longer. I won't be able to sleep, worrying.'

Rafael drummed his fingers on the table, wondering why he found her request so disturbing. Never in his life had he felt remotely protective about a woman. 'You're *not* seeing your father on your own.'

'I have to.' Her chin lifted and he gritted his teeth, contemplating the amount of work that awaited him.

Work that he'd ignored since the moment Grace Thacker

had landed in the rainforest with her high heels and her shiny blonde hair.

'All right.' Reluctantly he agreed. 'You can go home to London. But my plane is going to wait for you at the airport. You see your father, have the conversation you need to have and then come straight back here.'

Surprise lit her eyes. 'You mean that?'

'Yes. I want you to come back.' Why was she looking at him like that? Why wouldn't he want her to come back when the sex was so incredible?

CHAPTER TEN

TRYING not to be overawed by the luxury that surrounded her, Grace settled into her seat on Rafael's private jet for the long flight from Rio de Janeiro.

Once the staff had settled her onto the comfortable leather sofa, they presented her with a glass of champagne and a small package, elaborately wrapped, together with a note.

Her hands shaking, she opened the note first. *'You won't take gifts or money from me, but I hope you'll accept this. R.'*

"This" turned out to be a tiny tape recorder, small enough to fit into her pocket and with an earpiece. Intrigued and more than a little baffled by his choice of present, she switched it on and heard Rafael's voice summarising every nuance of the accounts. He covered everything they'd discussed, everything she needed to know and she felt the hot sting of tears behind her eyes as she realised just how long it must have taken him to record it and what such a gesture meant.

Maybe he didn't love her, but he certainly *cared.* He had to care, otherwise why would he go to so much trouble to help her?

Resolving to see her father so that she could return to the rainforest as soon as possible, she memorised everything on the tape and then slept for the remainder of the flight.

When they finally landed in London it was dark and drizzly

and she immediately wished she could climb straight back on the plane and return to the colour and richness of the rainforest.

Leaving the protection of his jet, she was ushered through a private section of the terminal reserved for VIPs and was enjoying the novelty of not having to elbow her way through throngs of stressed-out passengers, when something caught her attention.

Her face.

Staring out of the front of a newspaper.

For a moment she just stood, staring in silence at the picture of herself, and then she gave a soft moan of disbelief.

Appalled, she grabbed at it, reading the caption *'Cordeiro's new jungle love—see page 4 for full story.'*

Full story? What full story?

Her heart thudding against her chest, she rifled through the pages until she came to the page she wanted.

> Brazilian bad boy and billionaire Rafael Cordeiro has been playing jungle games with busty blonde business-woman Grace Thacker, owner of Café Brazil, a chain of coffee shops with outlets across London and the South East. A recluse since his costly divorce from actress Amber Naverin, Cordeiro was once quoted as saying that women were like garlic: 'nice at the time but left a bad taste in your mouth the day after.' Now he seems to be eating his words as he gets close and personal with yet another shapely blonde. According to her father, Patrick Thacker, Grace's small business is struggling so she's probably hoping for a generous cash injection from her new lover…

Unable to read any more, Grace stood for a moment, horror engulfing her in great, greedy waves.

Her father had sold the story to the Press. *But what story?* There was no story. She'd visited Rafael in the rainforest. What else was there to say, what else could they possibly know? Nothing. They'd been on their own, away from everyone. Wasn't that why he lived there, to escape this sort of thing?

Feeling sick, she forced herself to read the whole article and dropped the paper. Knowing nothing hadn't stopped them making wildly inaccurate claims designed to sell papers. But since when did anyone care about that?

A hot burst of anger gave way to horror and anxiety. Poor, poor Rafael. Would he think she'd been part of it? Maybe, maybe not, but it was exactly the sort of thing that he hated— part of the reason that he was so disillusioned. The thought that she'd been part of hurting him, even inadvertently, sickened her.

Functioning on automatic, she walked out of the airport towards the taxi rank, forgetting that she was supposed to meet up with Rafael's chauffeur in London.

Numb with misery and not thinking straight, she slipped into the back of a cab, trying to come to terms with the fact that yet again her father had done his best to hurt her.

Only this time he'd succeeded far better than he'd ever dreamed.

Because she knew that her relationship with Rafael was over. It had to be. What choice did she have? How could she expose him to this sort of scrutiny, knowing how fiercely he guarded his privacy?

Because of her, his name was all over the papers. Again.

And she'd never be able to control that, would she? If she continued her relationship with him, her father would always find some way of making money out of it. That was the sort of person he was.

And she loved Rafael far too much to let that happen.

Three days later, Rafael was pacing the length of the drawing room in his gated mansion, located in the most exclusive part of London.

Normally only a serious crisis in his business would have dragged him from the rainforest before he was ready to leave, but on this occasion he wasn't thinking about business. He was thinking about Grace.

The moment she'd left, he'd realised that he'd made a mistake letting her go. There was no way she should be confronting her father on her own.

He'd put in a call to his team in London, instructing them to keep her safely at his house until he arrived.

And that was when he'd discovered that she hadn't been seen since her arrival in London.

Trying to control his mounting temper, he turned again to the man standing nervously by the desk. 'Are you seriously telling me that she vanished?'

The man licked his lips. 'That's right, sir.'

'But she flew out of Rio on my plane,' Rafael pointed out in soft, deadly tones, 'so at what point, exactly, did you manage to lose her?'

The man swallowed. 'We're not honestly sure, sir. She was walking through the airport and then suddenly she wasn't there any more. She vanished.'

Cursing fluently in English and then reverting to his native Portuguese, Rafael thumped his fist onto the table and looked up with exasperation as another of his staff sidled into the room with a newspaper. '*Now* what?'

'We thought you ought to see this, sir.'

Rafael's eyes narrowed. 'I don't read tabloid newspapers.'

'I'm aware of that, sir.' The girl cleared her throat and stepped forward and thrust the newspaper towards him. 'But I think you'll want to read this one.'

Grace sat in the little park that was directly opposite the mews house that her father owned.

A week had passed since she'd read the story about herself in the paper and she'd spent the entire time thinking about what she could possibly do or say to make it up to Rafael.

In the end she'd sent a short note of apology and tried not to think of the luxurious private jet that had by now flown back to Rio without her.

Too upset to see her father as she'd planned, she'd checked herself into an anonymous bed and breakfast in an unfashionable part of London instead of returning to her flat. And she'd spent the whole of the last week staring up at the cream-painted ceiling of the small room, trying to work out what to do.

Trying to pull herself together.

It was over. And of course that was disappointing but it had always been going to finish at some point, hadn't it? Rafael didn't love her. He didn't love anyone, so their romantic interlude would have had a limited shelf life.

But none of the phrases going round in her head had offered even the smallest bit of comfort.

And finally the misery had faded and anger had taken its place.
Anger at her father for hurting Rafael.

It was funny, she thought numbly as she sat on the bench in the park, watching a mother strap a toddler into a pushchair, that two weeks ago she'd never even met the man and now here she was, struggling to work out a way of living her life without him.

And she would. Of course she would. She'd move on.

But she wasn't moving on until she'd spoken to her father.

For the first time in her life she was going to speak up and tell him how she felt. She had to. She had so much anger and hurt boiling up inside her that she didn't know what to do with it.

With a sigh that held both dread and resignation because she just *hated* confrontation, Grace stood up, walked across the park and then crossed the road to her father's house.

Daisy, her father's cleaner, opened the door. 'Oh, Miss

Thacker, where have you been?' She looked flustered. 'Your father's been so worried…'

Worried about what? That he'd finally been found out? Grace felt a dull ache bloom inside her. 'Is he in?'

'Well, yes, he is, but he has a visitor.' Daisy glanced nervously over her shoulder towards the study. 'Perhaps you should wait here and I'll tell him you're here.'

Grace heard raised voices and her stomach churned with nerves. And then she remembered that newspaper article and the anger rose inside her again. It was time to confront her father and she didn't care if she did it in public.

It had taken her a week to pluck up courage to come here. If she went away now, she'd never come back.

Ignoring Daisy's feeble attempts to stop her, Grace walked across the hall and walked straight into her father's study without bothering to knock.

Registering her father's white face and blustering attitude, she reflected idly that whoever he was talking to clearly had the upper hand. And then she turned and saw Rafael standing by the fireplace. His dark eyes bright with anger, every inch of his powerful frame simmering with a volcanic fury that heated the room.

What was he doing here?

Concern for him gave way to hideous embarrassment as she remembered the newspaper article and suddenly she wanted to turn and run. And maybe he detected that impulse because he crossed the room in two strides and grabbed her hands in his, holding them in an iron grip.

'You're not going anywhere—I know you hate confrontation but this is one situation that you're going to have to face because there are things that need to be said.'

How could she tell him that it wasn't the confrontation that was scaring her away, it was her guilt and embarrassment at seeing him after everything her father had done? 'I can understand that you're angry, but—'

'You're right that I'm angry. Never have I been so *furious* like this and the reason is *entirely* you.'

Wondering why his English suddenly seemed less than fluent when he was always so enviably eloquent in her language, Grace studied him, thinking that he looked incredibly tired. Had he been working through the night again? 'You've seen it, haven't you? That awful article. I was upset by it too and—'

'I'm not talking about the article. Do you really think I care about that? I'm angry because you completely disappeared from the face of the planet for an entire week and no one in the world seemed to know where you were! I'm on the verge of firing my entire London security team for being so inept!'

Her eyes widened. 'Rafael—'

'They lost you! I imagined you dead in a gutter somewhere, murdered by some lowlife that you trusted and saw good in…' His bronzed, handsome face had turned several shades paler and his hands tightened on her arms. *'Where have you been?'*

Still recovering from the shock of seeing him there, Grace didn't answer for a moment and he gave her a little shake.

'Do you have any idea how worried I've been? *Any idea at all?* I've had my entire security team pacing the streets of London looking for you for the past week.'

His blistering anger stunned her. 'You have?'

'Where were you? My flight crew assured me that you were safely delivered to the airport and then you just vanished. Why?'

Her mouth was dry. 'I saw the newspaper.'

'And?'

'And I just felt dreadful for you,' she muttered. 'I was *so* embarrassed. And so angry with my dad. I just couldn't face him until I'd had a chance to calm down a bit.'

'So why didn't you just fly straight back to Rio and calm down in my forest?'

Wasn't it obvious? 'Because there have been enough people in your life willing to sell their story to the papers. You don't need anyone else like that.'

His incredulous gaze raked her face. 'You had *nothing* to do with that story.'

'You believe that?' Ridiculously pleased, she gave a wobbly smile. 'Are you suddenly learning to trust, Rafael?'

His fingers tightened on her arms. 'No. Well, possibly, but only you,' he added hastily, drawing her against him. 'I *know* that story had nothing to do with you so why on earth did you suddenly go into hiding?'

'Because you don't need a man like my dad in your life!'

'That's enough from you, young lady!' Speaking for the first time, her father stepped forward, a scowl on his face. 'I'll have some respect when you speak about me. You both seem to have forgotten I'm here!'

She heard Rafael's sharp intake of breath but she pulled away from him and stepped towards her father. 'We haven't forgotten, Dad. Hardly. And as for giving you respect—' her voice shook as she looked at him, seeing for the first time the mean lines that pulled at his mouth, the coldness of his eyes '—respect is something that has to be earned. And you've never done that. You've never done a single thing in your life to warrant my respect.'

Her father gave a grunt of anger and his shoulders hunched. 'You watch your mouth, girl! No one talks back to me, especially not my own daughter. You're not too old for me to put my hand across your backside!'

Rafael stepped forward with a low growl of warning. 'Lay one finger on her and I'll send you somewhere you'll never need money again,' he promised in thickened tones and Grace put a hand on his arm in an instinctive gesture of restraint.

'You're not going to stop me from saying what needs to be said, Dad. I won't let you threaten me. I've had all week to prepare for this meeting and I've got things to say to you. And you're going to listen.'

Her father sneered. 'Oh, you're all very big and brave with your Brazilian bodyguard there, aren't you?'

Grace felt the mounting tension in Rafael's frame and kept her hand on his arm. 'You won't intimidate me. Not this time. Nor will you make me feel guilty. You've made a fortune from me. I know exactly how much, to the last penny. You *stole* from me—your own daughter,' just saying the words made her want to cry but she forced herself to plough on and say what needed to be said, knowing that if she didn't say it now then she might never have the courage again, 'and I've finally allowed myself to acknowledge the truth. You are *not* a good father and you never have been.'

Her father took a step towards her but must have caught something in Rafael's eyes because he suddenly stopped and simply glared. 'I did my best for you, Grace. You've always been difficult and ungrateful.'

'No.' She shook her head. 'I was neither of those things and you did not do your best for me. You did the best for *you*. You only ever thought about you. At school you didn't care about helping me, you just cared about your image. About what people would think about you having a daughter who couldn't even add up. And then when I started the business and I was doing so well, you weren't proud of me because you didn't care enough to be proud. You just exploited my weakness and you stripped my business bare. How could you do that, Daddy? *How could you?*'

Her father looked about to bluster his way out of it and then seemed to think better of it because he shrugged and then glanced at Rafael, a glint in his eyes. 'Well, I'm proud of you now. You've hit the jackpot, that's for sure. And good for you, Gracie, that's what I say.' He gave an unpleasant smile. 'We'll all benefit.'

Anger exploded inside her. 'No, you will not benefit from anything! How *dare* you take money from those innocent people? We were doing something good with Café Brazil, Dad. And you tainted it. You took food from the mouths of innocent people.'

Her father made an impatient sound. 'You always were a drama queen! Well, you've had your say so you can go now.'

'I haven't finished.' Her knees were shaking and she wasn't even aware that her fingers were digging into Rafael's arm. 'You stole from me, your daughter, and that's terrible, but the final straw for me, *the final straw,* was when you made money by talking about Rafael in the papers. *How could you stoop so low?*'

Her father shrugged dismissively. 'If the papers are willing to pay, let's give them a story, that's what I say.'

Grace turned away, distaste almost choking her. 'You have no morals. You are a greedy, sad little man who isn't even prepared to put the effort into making an honest living.'

'And you're so high and mighty!' Her father's temper finally exploded and he stepped towards her, his expression ugly. 'Why should I take a lesson on manners from a thick, stupid girl who can't even add up?'

In one stride Rafael reached him and punched him so hard that Patrick Thacker hit the wall with a sickening thud that made Grace gasp.

'Rafael, no! You mustn't.' She grabbed his arm, frightened by the volcanic fury she saw in his face, and he turned to her with disbelief, barely contained anger shimmering in his dark eyes.

'After everything he's done to you, you *still* care about him?'

'No.' She shook her head quickly and then hesitated and her narrow shoulders slumped. 'Well, yes, I suppose I do. He's still my father. His behaviour has been awful and that's really hard to come to terms with but he's family and—' she broke off and looked at her father, tears misting her gaze '—maybe I wasn't the easiest of daughters.'

'You're doing it again, making excuses for people,' Rafael growled, a frown on his face as he rubbed his bruised knuckles. 'You always do that. People throw bad at you and you sift through it looking for the one grain of good that might be lying at the bottom.'

'Yes—' her voice was choked '—well, that's who I am, Rafael. Sorry. Can't change the person inside, wasn't that what you told me? And anyway, if you hit him again you might seriously hurt him and I don't want you in trouble because of me.'

A faint smile touched his mouth. 'I'm already in trouble because of you, *meu amorzinho*,' he said softly, his accent suddenly very pronounced. 'Big trouble.'

Was he talking about seeing his name in the papers again? Unsure what he meant, Grace hesitated for a moment and then turned to her father, who was staggering to his feet, his hand pressed to his jaw. She stepped forward, blinking back tears. 'Don't even *think* about telling anyone about that punch or I'll come after you myself and punch you harder. And then I'll report you to the police for fraud.'

Her father moved his jaw gingerly. 'You'd never be able to prove it.'

'Why? Because I'm thick, stupid and I can't add up?' Her voice shook as she faced up to her father again. 'I can prove it, Dad. Print one story about Rafael and I will prove it.'

Her father stared at her. 'You wouldn't do that to your dad.'

'Actually I would.' She straightened her shoulders. 'You're still my dad and I love you, but I don't *like* you and I don't respect you. Somebody told me recently that I should toughen up and I've discovered that they're right. So I'm staying away from you until you've had time to think about what you've done. When you're ready to apologise, you can start with Rafael. Oh, and one more thing—' she lifted her chin '—the money that you made from that newspaper story. I want you to donate it to a charity for preserving the Brazilian rainforest.'

And then she felt Rafael's fingers close around her wrist and allowed him to lead her from the room.

Curled up on the sofa in Rafael's luxurious home in Mayfair, Grace stared sightlessly at the painting on the wall.

After her confrontation with her father, Rafael had virtually dragged her into the comfort of his limousine and instructed the driver to take them to his house. And now she'd been sitting on her own for ten minutes while he answered a pressing phone call.

'I'm sorry to leave you like that…' Rafael strode back into the room and cursed softly as he saw her sitting so still. '*Stop* thinking about him! He isn't worth it.'

She stirred and looked at him. 'How did you know I was thinking about him?'

'Because it's obvious. Knowing you, you're sitting there trying to make excuses for your father's *appalling* behaviour.' He spread his hands in a gesture of exasperation and strode across to her, sitting on the edge of the sofa and taking her hand in his. 'There is no excuse. You should have let me punch him again and then you should have told him that he was out of your life.'

Grace shook her head. 'I couldn't do that,' she muttered. 'He's still my dad.'

Rafael let out a stream of unintelligible Portuguese and eventually switched to English. 'You are incredible, no? Your father tries to destroy you and what do you do? You tell him that you love him! He doesn't deserve your love!'

'Everyone deserves to be loved.' Grace wiped the tears away with the tips of her fingers and Rafael cursed softly and sat down on the sofa next to her.

'You're *very* upset, but now you must forget him for the time being.'

'Yes.' She managed a smile. 'Sorry about this. You hate emotions and you've been subjected to a bucketload today. Newspaper stores, arguments with my father, emotional scenes. It must be your worst nightmare. How's your hand?'

'It's fine and none of that amounts to anything when compared with the stress of the last week,' he assured her, reaching across and pulling her onto his lap. 'The moment you left I realised that I shouldn't have let you go. There was no way you should have had to face your father on your own.'

'It was my fight, Rafael.' But she didn't feel like fighting now and she snuggled on his lap, taking the comfort that he offered.

'You're not built for fighting. You don't have an aggressive bone in your body. The moment you left I knew I'd made a mistake letting you go alone.'

'Is that why you came after me?'

'Yes.' Rafael slipped his fingers under her chin and lifted her face to his. 'I couldn't stand the thought of you facing your father and then I discovered that you'd disappeared.'

'When I saw that newspaper, I was terribly upset.' She bit her lip. 'Sorry. I know you don't like emotional discussions, but you have no idea what it feels like to be completely let down by the only family you have.' There was a long, throbbing silence and she felt him tense against her.

'Actually, I do,' he said hoarsely. 'I know exactly what it's like.'

She sat up straight on his lap so that she could see his face. 'I thought you didn't have a family? Are you telling me that your father let you down?'

'My father let me down before I was born by leaving my mother to bring me up alone.' He shifted her off his lap and rose to his feet, his shoulders tense as he strode across the room to the window. 'Until I was eight years old she raised me on her own.'

Sensing instinctively that those demons were finally about to reveal their shape, Grace watched as he stared down into the street below. 'You've never mentioned your mother before. You lived in Rio?' Her gentle prompt made him turn.

'Yes.' His eyes glittered hard and cold. 'In one tiny room, with barely enough space for one person to live, let alone two. It was a miserable existence. And then my mother met a new man.'

'She fell in love?'

He gave a faint smile and there was mockery in his eyes as they lingered on her face. 'Always the romantic, aren't you? No, *meu amorzinho,* it wasn't love. But he was very wealthy and she saw how marriage to him would significantly improve her lifestyle. There was only one problem. He wasn't prepared to take on someone else's child.'

Shocked, Grace stared at him. 'He told you that?'

'I overheard them talking.' He stuffed his hands in his pockets. 'They were in the process of arranging for me to go into a local children's home.'

Grace shook her head in an instinctive denial of what was coming. 'She didn't mean that, surely,' she said softly. 'Perhaps she thought if she said that then he'd come round and make you a family.'

'He didn't want a family, Grace. Or at least, not someone else's.'

'Your mother put you in a children's home?'

'No. I didn't let them do that. I left home.' He gave a smile of self-mockery. 'You see? Even at the tender age of eight, I was determined to be in control of my own destiny. There was no way I was just going to let life happen to me.'

'But you were *eight years old.*' She lifted both hands to her face and shook her head, unable to bear the thought of him alone at such a young age. 'How can you take charge of your destiny at eight years old? What did you do? Where did you go?'

'I stole money from his wallet and then I packed a bag and climbed on a bus. I went as far as the money would take me.' His tone was flat and without a trace of emotion. 'I climbed off the bus and I stood by the side of the road, wondering what on earth I'd done. I suddenly realised I had nothing to eat or drink and nowhere to sleep.'

Grace's eyes filled. 'You must have been so afraid and so lonely.'

'Well, I realised that if I stayed by the side of the road then someone might well pick me up and return me to Rio. So I walked into the rainforest.'

'The rainforest?' She stared at him, appalled, remembering her own experience in similar surroundings. 'You wandered into the rainforest on your own and you were only eight? But that's so dangerous. Snakes, spiders—'

'I was never bothered about snakes and spiders but I hated the ants and the noises bothered me at first.'

'At first? *How long did you stay in the rainforest?*'

'A month.'

She rose to her feet. 'You lived in the forest on your own for a whole month? But you were just a child, Rafael; how did you do it? What did you eat, drink?'

He shrugged. 'I ate fruit. Berries. Drank water that I probably shouldn't have drunk but it didn't do me any harm. It's true that I was a great deal thinner by the time they eventually found me.'

'Your mother found you?'

He gave a twisted smile. 'Oh, no. I doubt she ever bothered looking. She was, I'm sure, extremely relieved to have had the problem removed from her life.'

'So if your mother didn't find you, then who did?'

'Carlos.'

'Carlos who owns the *fazenda?*'

'That's right. I'd strayed onto his land. He took me home to Filomena. They fed me, gave me some clean clothes because mine were pretty filthy by then and gradually drew the story out of me.'

'But they didn't send you away?'

'Oh, no, they didn't do that. They took me in and I never left.'

It explained so much about him. 'So that's why you love them so much,' she whispered and he gave a faint frown as if he hadn't considered the nature of the bond before.

'I owe them everything. They gave me a home and security.'

'But they couldn't make up for what your mother had done.' Grace walked towards him, her hands outstretched. 'It's no wonder you don't trust women. It isn't just about your ex-wife, is it? It started a long, long time before that. And you were so, *so* young.'

He hesitated and then took her hands. 'I suppose at a very young, impressionable age I was given the message that a woman will do just about anything if the price is right. Even give away her child. Amber's behaviour was simply more of the same; she used pregnancy as a lever to get me to marry her. I never had any reason to change my view of women.' His eyes found hers. 'Until I met you. I owe you an apology.'

Her eyes widened. 'For what?'

'For not believing that you were innocent.' His fingers tightened on her hands. 'The thing is, Grace, I'd never actually come across truth and innocence before, so when I finally did I didn't recognise it.'

'You have *nothing* to apologise for.'

'I hurt you by not believing in you. And I hurt you by not using romantic words when I took you to bed.' He cursed softly and hauled her against him. 'I'm useless with emotions, Grace. It's like another language. I just don't know any of the right words. You're going to have to teach me.'

Her heart thudded against her chest and she shook her head and covered his lips with her fingers. 'Don't. Don't say that,' she urged softly. 'It's fine. It doesn't matter. I know you can't say the words and I know you don't do commitment but I'm yours for as long as you want me. We don't have to talk at all if you don't want to.'

His eyes glittered. 'You'd do that? You'd stay with me without any sort of commitment?'

'Of course. How can you doubt it?' She brushed her fingers over his brow. 'I just want to be with you. I love you, Rafael. And I don't expect you to love me back, but I want the chance to make you happy for as long as you'll let me.'

He was still. 'You love me?'

'Of course. How can you even ask that?'

'But you didn't come back to Rio. You vanished for a week. If I hadn't tracked you down you would have been out of my life.'

'Because that's what I thought was best for you. My father will always cause problems between us.'

'Forget about your father.' He studied her face. 'Why would you stay with me? What do you get from me in return?'

She smiled. 'I get to see parrots and butterflies, I get to swim in a forest pool but most of all I get to sleep alongside a man who makes me feel like a woman for the first time in my life.'

His eyes were full of dark shadows. 'I ought to be telling you to run. I ought to be telling you that I won't be good for you because I've never been good for anyone in my life. But I'm too selfish for any of that. I want you. And I always go after what I want.'

'And I'm glad you do. Telling me to run wouldn't make a difference, anyway. I'm not leaving until you've had enough of me. And I know you haven't.'

'I'll never have enough of you.' He took her face in his hands and stood looking at her for so long that she started to feel nervous.

'What? What's the matter?'

He didn't reply and his breathing was unsteady, as if he was dragging something out from deep inside himself.

She frowned. 'Rafael? What's wrong?'

'I love you, too.' He spoke the words hesitantly, with none of his usual confidence. And she felt her heart perform a series of elaborate acrobatics in her chest. 'I never thought I'd say those words to anyone. I never thought I was capable of feeling love. But I am. With you.'

She opened her mouth but he shook his head.

'Don't interrupt me,' he said hoarsely, a flash of humour in his eyes. 'I've never done this before so I might get it wrong if you interrupt me.'

Grace didn't feel capable of speaking so she just stood, trapped in a bubble of happiness as she listened.

'You arrived in my forest and you were so gutsy and optimistic. You were prepared to fly all that way to try and talk me into saving your business and no matter what I did or said, how horrid I was, you seemed to find it impossible to see bad in me.'

'I didn't see bad in you,' she said quietly. 'I saw pain and disillusionment. But nothing bad.'

'You tramped through the rainforest without a word of complaint—'

'I loved it—'

'And then you came to my bed...' He looked her direct in the eye and let his hands drop to his sides. 'You were a virgin, weren't you?'

Colour bloomed in her cheeks and she opened her mouth and closed it again.

He rubbed his fingers over the bridge of his nose and gave a soft curse. 'I thought so. It took a few days for it to sink in but then it did. Why did you do it, Grace? Why did you give so much?'

That was easy to answer. 'Because I wanted to. I think I fell in love with you almost immediately even though I knew that didn't make sense. I just wanted to be with you. In every way possible. I didn't care about the consequences.'

'I've never met anyone like you before,' he muttered, sliding his arms round her again and hauling her against him. 'You are so incredibly generous and you take nothing back.'

'Yes, I do.' There was humour in her eyes as she looked up at him. 'I made you sit with me for hours going through numbers. For most people that would have been torture.'

'Not for me,' he assured her, lowering his head and capturing her mouth with his in a brief but devastating kiss. 'You do realise, don't you, that I'm not going to let you go?'

'You're not?'

'No.' He lifted her hands and she felt him slide something onto her finger.

'What's that? Oh—' She stared in amazement at the huge diamond that now adorned her hand and tears filled her eyes. 'I told you, I didn't want jewellery.'

'It isn't jewellery,' he informed her in a tone that sounded more like himself, 'it's a statement of possession. My corporate branding. It tells the world that you're mine. Don't ever take it off.'

She touched it in awe, confused by what it meant. 'You're asking me to wear your ring?'

'I'm asking you to marry me,' he said softly. 'You've given me so much already, but I want more and I want it forever.'

She felt the hot sting of tears behind her eyes. 'What have I ever given you? Thanks to my father I don't have any money and I can't even add up—'

'I can add up for both of us and I have more money than we will ever possibly need.' He brushed a stray tear away from her cheek with his thumb. 'You seriously don't know what you've given me? Then let me tell you, Grace. You gave me your trust when I didn't deserve it and unconditional love, which is something that no one has ever given me before. You saw good in me when I only showed you the bad. And you've given me hope.'

She swallowed. 'Rafael—'

'I love you…' He gave a wolfish smile. 'There; it's getting easier to say all the time with practice. I love you.'

She smiled through her tears. 'I love you too. So much.'

'Good.' He lowered his mouth to hers. 'How would you feel about an extended honeymoon in the rainforest?'

BILLIONAIRES' BRIDES

by Sandra Marton

Pregnant by their princes...

Take three incredibly wealthy European princes
and match them with three beautiful, spirited women.
Add large helpings of intense emotion and passionate attraction.
Result: three unexpected pregnancies...and
three possible princesses—if those princes have their way....

THE ITALIAN PRINCE'S PREGNANT BRIDE
August 2007

THE GREEK PRINCE'S CHOSEN WIFE
September 2007

THE SPANISH PRINCE'S VIRGIN BRIDE

Prince Lucas Reyes believes Alyssa is trying to pretend
she's untouched by any man. Lucas's fiery royal blood is roused!
He'd swear she's pure uninhibited mistress material,
and never a virgin bride!

Available October wherever you buy books.

Look for more great Harlequin authors every month!

HARLEQUIN®

Mediterranean NIGHTS™

*Sail aboard the luxurious Alexandra's Dream and
experience glamour, romance, mystery and revenge!*

Coming in October 2007...

AN AFFAIR TO REMEMBER

by

Karen Kendall

When Captain Nikolas Pappas first fell in love with
Helena Stamos, he was a penniless deckhand and she
was the daughter of a shipping magnate. But he's
never forgiven himself for the way he left her—and
fifteen years later, he's determined to win her back.

Though the attraction is still there, Helena is hesitant
to get involved. Nick left her once...what's to stop
him from doing it again?

REQUEST YOUR FREE BOOKS!

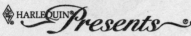 HARLEQUIN® *Presents*®

2 FREE NOVELS PLUS 2 FREE GIFTS!

PASSION
GUARANTEED
SEDUCTION

YES! Please send me 2 FREE Harlequin Presents® novels and my 2 FREE gifts. After receiving them, if I don't wish to receive any more books, I can return the shipping statement marked "cancel." If I don't cancel, I will receive 6 brand-new novels every month and be billed just $3.80 per book in the U.S., or $4.47 per book in Canada, plus 25¢ shipping and handling per book and applicable taxes, if any*. That's a savings of close to 15% off the cover price! I understand that accepting the 2 free books and gifts places me under no obligation to buy anything. I can always return a shipment and cancel at any time. Even if I never buy another book from Harlequin, the two free books and gifts are mine to keep forever.

106 HDN EEXK 306 HDN EEXV

Name _____ (PLEASE PRINT)

Address _____ Apt. #

City _____ State/Prov. _____ Zip/Postal Code

Signature (if under 18, a parent or guardian must sign)

Mail to the **Harlequin Reader Service®**:
IN U.S.A.: P.O. Box 1867, Buffalo, NY 14240-1867
IN CANADA: P.O. Box 609, Fort Erie, Ontario L2A 5X3

Not valid to current Harlequin Presents subscribers.

Want to try two free books from another line?
Call 1-800-873-8635 or visit www.morefreebooks.com.

* Terms and prices subject to change without notice. NY residents add applicable sales tax. Canadian residents will be charged applicable provincial taxes and GST. This offer is limited to one order per household. All orders subject to approval. Credit or debit balances in a customer's account(s) may be offset by any other outstanding balance owed by or to the customer. Please allow 4 to 6 weeks for delivery.

Your Privacy: Harlequin is committed to protecting your privacy. Our Privacy Policy is available online at www.eHarlequin.com or upon request from the Reader Service. From time to time we make our lists of customers available to reputable firms who may have a product or service of interest to you. If you would prefer we not share your name and address, please check here. ☐

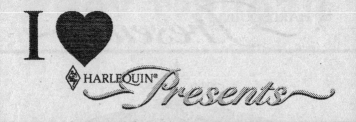

Always passionate, always proud.

**The richest royal family in the world—
a family united by blood and passion,
torn apart by deceit and desire.**

By royal decree, Harlequin Presents is delighted to bring
you The Royal House of Niroli. Step into the glamorous,
enticing world of the Nirolian royal family. As the king
ails he must find an heir…each month an exciting new
installment follows the epic search for the true Nirolian
king. Eight heirs, eight romances, eight fantastic stories!

THE TYCOON'S
PRINCESS BRIDE
by Natasha Oakley

Isabella can't be in the same room as Domenic Vincini
without wanting him! But if she gives in to temptation
she forfeits her chance of being queen…and will tie
Niroli to its sworn enemy!
Available October wherever you buy books.

Be sure not to miss any of the passion!
EXPECTING HIS ROYAL BABY
by Susan Stephens
available in November.